MAKTUB

ALSO BY PAULO COELHO

The Alchemist

The Pilgrimage

The Valkyries

By the River Piedra I Sat Down and Wept

The Fifth Mountain

Veronika Decides to Die

Warrior of the Light: A Manual

Eleven Minutes

The Zahir

The Devil and Miss Prym

The Witch of Portobello

Brida

The Winner Stands Alone

Aleph

Manuscript Found in Accra

Adultery

The Spy

Hippie

The Archer

MAKTUB

PAULO COELHO

An Inspirational Companion to

THE ALCHEMIST

Translated from the Portuguese by Margaret Jull Costa

HARPERONE
An Imprint of HarperCollins*Publishers*

HarperCollins books may be purchased for educational, business, or sales promotional use. For information, please email the Special Markets Department at SPsales@harpercollins.com.

Originally published as *Maktub* in Brazil in 1994 by Rocco.

FIRST HARPERONE HARDCOVER PUBLISHED IN 2024

Designed by Michele Cameron
Illustrations © Oliska/Shutterstock

Library of Congress Cataloging-in-Publication Data has been applied for.

ISBN 978-0-06-334654-3
ISBN 978-0-06-339654-8 (ANZ)

23 24 25 26 27 LBC 5 4 3 2 1

O Mary, conceived without sin, pray for us who have recourse to thee. Amen.

For Nhá Chica, Patrícia Casé, Edinho,
and Alcino Leite Neto

I thank thee, O Father, Lord of heaven and earth,
that thou hast hid these things from the wise and prudent,
and hast revealed them unto babes.

Luke 10:21, KJV

Before We Begin

MAKTUB IS NOT A BOOK offering advice. It is an exchange of experiences.

Much of it consists of my master's teachings over the eleven long years we have known each other. Other stories were given to me by friends or people whom I met only once but who left me with an unforgettable message. Finally, there are the books I've read and the stories that—as the Jesuit Anthony de Mello says—belong to the spiritual heritage of the human race.

Maktub was born out of a phone call from Alcino Leite Neto, then editor of the *Folha de São Paulo* color supplement. I was in the United States at the time, and I agreed to his proposal for a daily column with no clear idea about what I would write. I found the challenge exciting, though, and decided to go ahead with it; after all, to live means to take risks.

When I realized how much work was involved, I have to say that I almost gave up. What with frequent trips abroad to promote my books, the daily column became a real torment. However, all the signs were telling me to carry on: a letter from a reader, a comment made by a friend, someone showing me the clippings she had kept in her purse.

Slowly, I learned how to be more objective and direct in what I wrote. I had to do a lot of rereading, something I had always put off, but revisiting these stories brought me huge pleasure.

I began to take more careful note of my master's words. I began to look at everything happening around me as another reason to write *Maktub*, and I found all this so enriching that, today, I am grateful to have had this daily task.

For this book, I have selected stories published in *Folha de São Paulo* between June 10, 1993, and June 11, 1994. Others were published in *Warrior of the Light*, and both *Maktub* and *Warrior of the Light* can be read as companions to *The Alchemist*.

In the preface to one of his books of stories, Anthony de Mello says this about the author's role: "His task has been that of the weaver and the dyer. He takes no credit at all for the cotton and the thread."

Neither do I.

Paulo Coelho

THE TRAVELER IS SITTING IN the middle of the countryside looking at the modest house in front of him. He had been there before with friends, but all he had noticed then was the similarity between the style of that house and the style of a Catalan architect who had lived a long time ago and had never set foot in that place.

The house is close to Cabo Frio, in Rio de Janeiro, and is entirely built of discarded fragments. In 1899, its owner, Gabriel, had a dream in which an angel told him: "Build a house out of fragments." Gabriel began collecting cracked tiles, plates, ornaments, and broken pots. "Every fragment transformed into something beautiful," Gabriel said of his work. For the first forty years, the locals decided he must be mad, but when a few tourists discovered the house and began bringing their friends, then Gabriel became a genius. The novelty soon wore off, however, and Gabriel was once again relegated to anonymity. Nevertheless, he continued building

MAKTUB

his house, and when he was ninety-three, he put the final shard of glass in place and died.

The traveler lights a cigarette and smokes in silence. Today, he isn't thinking about the similarity between Gabriel's house and the architecture of Antoni Gaudí. He is looking at all those fragments and reflecting on his own existence, which, like that of everyone else, is made up of fragments of everything that has happened to him. At a certain point, though, those fragments begin to take shape.

And the traveler recalls a little of his past life as he reads the papers he is holding. These are fragments of his life too: experiences he lived through, unforgettable passages from books, his master's teachings, stories told to him by friends or by others, as well as reflections on his own times and on the dreams of his generation.

Just like the man who dreamed that an angel visited him and then went on to build the house the traveler is looking at now, he is trying to put those papers in order so as to understand his own spiritual architecture. He remembers, as a child, reading a book by Malba Tahan entitled *Maktub!*, and he thinks:

"Perhaps I should do the same."

PAULO COELHO

THE MASTER SAYS:

When we sense that the time has come to change, we begin—unconsciously—to rerun a tape showing all our failures up until then.

And of course, as we grow older, our quota of difficult moments increases too. However, at the same time, experience has given us the means to overcome those defeats and find a path that will allow us to carry on. We need to include that on our mental video as well.

If we only watch the video of our failures, we will become paralyzed and unable to act. If we only watch the video of our successes, we will end up thinking we are much wiser than we really are.

We need both videos.

MAKTUB

IMAGINE A CATERPILLAR. He spends much of his life on the ground, looking up at the birds, filled with indignation at both his fate and his appearance. "I am the most despicable of creatures," he thinks. "Ugly, repulsive, condemned to crawl about on the earth."

One day, though, Nature asks him to make a cocoon. The caterpillar is most alarmed; he has never made a cocoon before. He assumes he is building his own tomb and prepares to die. Still indignant at the life he has led so far, he again complains to God:

"Just when I'd finally gotten used to being me, You take away the little I have."

In despair, he shuts himself up in the cocoon and awaits his end.

A few days later, though, he finds he has been transformed into a beautiful butterfly. He can fly about in the air and be admired by humans. He is surprised by the direction in which life has taken him and by God's designs.

PAULO COELHO

A STRANGER WENT to see the abbot of the Scetis monastery.

"I want to lead a better life," he said, "but I can't stop thinking about sinful things."

Noticing that it was windy outside, the abbot said to the stranger:

"It's very hot in here. Could you grab a piece of that wind and bring it in here to cool the room?"

"That's impossible," said the stranger.

"Just as impossible as it is to stop thinking about things that might offend God," said the abbot. "But if you can say no to temptations, they won't cause you any trouble."

MAKTUB

THE MASTER SAYS:

Whenever there is a decision to be made, it's best just to go ahead and accept the consequences. You cannot possibly know in advance what those consequences might be.

The art of divination was intended to advise humankind, not to foresee the future. Divination is an excellent counselor, but a terrible prophet.

In the prayer that Jesus taught us, He says: "Thy will be done." Whenever that will presents us with a problem, it always brings with it the solution.

If the art of divination had ever succeeded in seeing into the future, every diviner would be rich, married, and content.

PAULO COELHO

THE DISCIPLE WENT to see his master.

"For years now I have sought enlightenment," he said. "I feel I am very close now, but I want to know what my next step should be."

"How do you earn your living?" asked the master.

"I've never yet had to earn my living, because my mother and father have always supported me, but that's a mere detail."

"Your next step is to look at the sun for half a minute," said the master.

The disciple obeyed.

When he had done as he was told, he was asked by the master to describe the countryside around him.

"I can't see a thing, because the sun blinded me," said the disciple.

"A man who seeks only the light and hands all his responsibilities to others will never find enlightenment. A man who keeps his eyes fixed only on the sun will end up blind," said the master.

MAKTUB

A MAN WAS walking along a valley in the Pyrenees when he met an old shepherd. He shared his food with him, and they talked for a long time about life.

The man said that, if he were to believe in God, he would also have to believe that he had no free will, since God would govern his every step.

The shepherd then took him to a mountain pass, where every sound came back to them in the form of a perfectly clear echo.

"Life is like the walls of this mountain pass, and fate is the cry of each and every person," said the shepherd. "Whatever we do will be carried up to God's heart and returned to us in kind. God acts as the echo of our actions."

PAULO COELHO

MAKTUB MEANS "IT is written." To Arabic speakers, though, this is not the best translation because, even if everything has already been written, God is merciful and only uses His pen and ink to help us.

The traveler is in New York. He wakes up late for an appointment, and when he goes out into the street, he finds that his car has been towed away by the police.

He arrives at his meeting late, lunch drags on for longer than necessary, and he's worried about the fine. It will cost him a fortune. Suddenly, he remembers the dollar bill he found the previous day. He makes a crazy connection between the dollar bill and what happened that morning. "Perhaps I picked up the bill before it could be found by the person it was intended for. Perhaps I removed it from the path of someone who really needed it. Perhaps I interfered with what was written."

He needs to get rid of it, and at that very moment, he sees

a beggar sitting on the sidewalk. He quickly hands him the dollar bill.

"Just a moment," says the beggar. "I'm a poet, and I want to repay you with a poem."

"Make it short, because I'm in a hurry," says the traveler.

The beggar says:

"If you're still alive, that's because you haven't yet reached the place you're supposed to reach."

PAULO COELHO

THE DISCIPLE SAID to his master:

"I've spent much of the day thinking things I shouldn't think, wanting things I shouldn't want, and making plans I shouldn't make."

The master invited the disciple to go for a walk in the woods near his house. On the way, he pointed to a plant and asked his disciple if he knew what it was.

"Belladonna," said his disciple. "It can kill you if you eat the leaves."

"But it can't kill you if you just look at it," said his master. "In the same way, negative thoughts can't harm you as long as you don't allow yourself to be seduced by them."

MAKTUB

A CHAIN OF mountains separates France and Spain. At the foot of those mountains is a village called Argelès, and in that village is a hill that leads down into the valley.

Every afternoon, an old man goes up and down that hill.

When the traveler went to Argelès for the first time, he didn't really notice this. The second time, he did notice that he always passed the same old man. And each time he visited the village, he picked out more details: the man's clothes, his beret, his walking stick, his glasses. Now, whenever he thinks about that village, he also thinks about the old man, who of course is quite unaware of this.

Only once did the traveler speak to him, asking in a jokey way:

"Do you think God lives in these lovely mountains all around us?"

"God," said the old man, "lives wherever people allow Him in."

PAULO COELHO

THE MASTER MET up with his disciples one night and asked them to build a fire so that they could sit around it and talk.

"The spiritual path is like that fire," he said. "Anyone lighting a fire first has to put up with a lot of dreadful smoke that irritates their lungs and makes their eyes water. Rediscovering one's faith is the same. However, once the fire is lit, the smoke disappears, and the flames light up everything, bringing us warmth and peace."

"And what if someone lights the fire for us?" asked one of the disciples. "And what if someone helps us to avoid the smoke?"

"Anyone who does that is not a true master because he can take the fire wherever he wishes or put it out whenever he wants. And since he hasn't taught anyone how to light the fire, he could easily leave the whole world in darkness."

MAKTUB

A FRIEND OF mine decided to take her three children and go and live on a small farm in a remote part of Canada.

She wanted to devote herself entirely to spiritual contemplation.

In less than a year, she had fallen in love, remarried, studied the meditation techniques of the saints, campaigned for a school for her children to be built, made friends, made enemies, neglected her teeth, developed an abscess, hitched a ride in the middle of a snowstorm, and learned how to repair her car, unfreeze the pipes, make her alimony money last until the end of the month, live off benefits, sleep in an unheated house, laugh for no reason, weep tears of despair, build a chapel, do DIY jobs around the house, paint walls, and give courses on spirituality.

"I came to understand that a life of prayer doesn't mean a life lived in isolation," she says. "God's love is so great that it needs to be shared."

PAULO COELHO

"WHEN YOU FIRST set off on your path, you will find a door with some words painted on it," says the master. "Come back and tell me what those words are."

The disciple puts heart and soul into looking for that door. One day, he sees it and returns to his master.

"At the beginning of the path, the sign said: 'This is impossible.'"

"Where was that written, on a wall or a door?" asks the master.

"On a door," says the disciple.

"Well, grab the handle and open the door."

The disciple obeys. Since the words are painted on the door, they move when the door moves, and when the door stands wide open, the disciple can no longer see the words and so continues on his way.

MAKTUB

THE MASTER SAYS:

Close your eyes. No, you don't even need to close your eyes. Simply imagine this scene: a flock of birds in full flight. Right, tell me how many birds you can see. Five? Eleven? Seventeen?

Whatever your answer—and it's hard for anyone to give a precise number—one thing is clear from this small experiment. You were perfectly capable of imagining a flock of birds, but the number of birds was not in your control. And yet the scene was so clear and defined and exact. The answer to the question lies elsewhere.

Who decided how many birds would appear in that scene? Not you.

PAULO COELHO

A MAN DECIDED to visit a hermit who lived near the Scetis monastery. After wandering aimlessly about the desert, he finally found him.

"I need to know what should be my first step on the spiritual path," he said.

The hermit led him to a small pool and asked him to look at his own reflection in the water. The man obeyed, but the hermit started throwing pebbles in the water, making the surface ripple.

"I won't be able to see my face clearly if you keep throwing pebbles in the water," said the man.

"Just as it is impossible for a man to see his own face in choppy waters, so it is impossible to seek God if the mind is too focused on the search," said the monk. "That is the first step."

MAKTUB

DURING THE TIME when the traveler was practicing Zen Buddhist meditation, there was a moment when the master went over to a corner of the dojo and returned wielding a bamboo stick.

Some students—who had failed to focus on their meditation—raised their hand, and the master struck them three times on each shoulder.

Initially, this seemed absurdly medieval.

Later, the traveler realized that it is sometimes necessary to place spiritual pain on a physical level so that you can actually feel the damage it does. On the road to Santiago, he learned another exercise, which consisted of sticking the nail of his index finger into his thumb whenever he had some negative thought.

PAULO COELHO

It often takes a long time to notice the terrible consequences of negative thoughts. By having those thoughts manifest themselves in the form of physical pain, we come to understand the damage they do.

And we begin to avoid them.

MAKTUB

A THIRTY-TWO-YEAR-OLD PATIENT went to see the therapist Richard Crowley.

"I can't stop sucking my thumb," he said.

"Don't worry about that," said Crowley, "but try sucking a different finger on each day of the week."

From that moment on, whenever the patient raised his hand to his mouth, he was obliged to choose which finger he would suck that day. Before the week was out, he was cured.

"When something bad becomes a habit, it's hard to deal with," says Richard Crowley. "However, when these challenges require us to adopt new attitudes, make new decisions and choices, then we realize that bad habits are simply not worth the effort."

PAULO COELHO

IN ANCIENT ROME, a group of witches known as Sibyls wrote nine books foretelling the future of Rome. They took the nine books to Tiberius, the Roman emperor.

"How much do they cost?" asked Tiberius.

"One hundred gold coins," answered the Sibyls.

Outraged, Tiberius sent them away. The Sibyls burned three of the books and returned.

"They still cost one hundred gold coins," they said.

Tiberius laughed but refused their offer. Why pay the same price for six books as he would for nine?

The Sibyls burned another three books and returned with the remaining three.

"They still cost one hundred gold coins," they said.

By then, Tiberius's curiosity was aroused, and he ended up paying the full amount, except then, of course, he could only

MAKTUB

21

read some of what they had predicted for the future of his empire.

The master says:

Part of the art of living is knowing not to try and haggle with any opportunities that present themselves.

THESE WORDS WERE written by Rufus Jones, one of the most influential Quakers of the twentieth century:

"I have no interest in building new towers of Babel with, as my excuse, the idea that I need to reach God.

"Those towers are abominations; some are made out of concrete and bricks, others out of piles of sacred texts. Some were built out of ancient rituals, and many are constructed out of new scientific evidence proving the existence of God.

"All these towers, which we have to climb from a dark, solitary base, may offer us a view of the Earth, but they do not lead us up to Heaven.

"All we get is the same old confusion of languages and emotions.

"The bridges to God are faith, love, joy, and prayer."

MAKTUB

TWO RABBIS WERE doing their utmost to bring spiritual comfort to the Jews in Nazi Germany. Despite living in constant fear for their own lives, for two years they managed to elude their pursuers and held religious services in various Jewish communities.

In the end, they were caught. One of the rabbis spent all his time praying, terrified about what might happen to them. The other rabbi spent all day sleeping.

"Why are you sleeping so much?" asked the frightened rabbi.

"To conserve my energy, because I know I'm going to need it," said the other rabbi.

"Aren't you afraid? Don't you know what might happen to us?"

"I *was* afraid until they put us in prison. Now that I'm a prisoner, what's the point of fearing what has already happened? The time for being afraid is over; now begins the time for hoping."

PAULO COELHO

THE MASTER SAYS:

"I don't want to." We should treat these words with some suspicion.

What are the things we don't want to do because we don't want to, and what are the things we don't want to do simply because they seem too risky?

Here's one example: speaking to strangers. Whether it's a real conversation, a brief chat, or a heart-to-heart, we rarely speak to strangers.

And we always feel that "it is better that way."

We end up neither helping nor being helped by Life.

Keeping a distance from others makes us seem more important, more confident. In practice, though, we're not allowing the voice of our angel to manifest itself in the mouths of others.

MAKTUB

AN OLD HERMIT was once invited to the court of the most powerful king of the day.

"I envy a holy man who can be contented with so little," said the king.

"I envy Your Majesty who can be contented with even less than me," answered the hermit.

"How can you say that when this whole country belongs to me?" said the king, somewhat offended.

"Precisely," said the old man. "I have the music of the spheres, I have the rivers and the mountains of the whole world, I have the moon and the sun, because I have God in my soul. Your Majesty, on the other hand, only has this kingdom."

PAULO COELHO

"LET'S GO UP to the mountain where God lives," said a knight to his fellow knight. "I want to prove that all He ever does is ask *us* to do things, while never doing anything to lighten our load."

"I will go there in order to show my faith," said the other knight.

They reached the top of the mountain when night had already fallen, and they heard a Voice in the darkness:

"Get back on your horses, but take with you those stones on the ground!"

"You see?" said the first knight. "We've come all this way, and now He just wants us to carry more weight. Well, I won't do it!"

The second knight did as the Voice instructed. By the time they reached the bottom of the mountain, day was breaking, and the first rays of sun were glinting on the stones the devout knight had brought down with him. They were diamonds.

The master says:

God may make strange decisions, but they are always in our favor.

THE MASTER SAYS:

My dear friend, I have some news that you may not have heard. I thought I should try and soften the blow and paint the news in bright colors, filling it with promises of Paradise, visions of the Absolute, and other esoteric explanations, but although all those things do exist, they are not relevant now.

Take a deep breath and prepare yourself. I must speak frankly, and I can assure you that I know that what I'm about to say is true. It is an infallible prediction with no margin for error.

The news is this: you are going to die.

It might be tomorrow or in fifty years' time, but sooner or later, you will die. Even if you don't want to. Even if you have other plans.

Think carefully about what you will do today. And tomorrow. And for the rest of your days.

MAKTUB

A WHITE EXPLORER, eager to reach his destination in the heart of Africa, paid his native bearers extra so that they would walk more quickly. For several days, they did just that.

One afternoon, though, they all sat down on the ground, took off the bundles they were carrying, and refused to go on. Regardless of how much money the explorer offered them, they would not move. When he finally asked the reason for their behavior, he received this reply:

"We've been walking so fast that we no longer know what we're doing. Now we need to wait for our souls to catch up with us."

PAULO COELHO

Our Lady, with the Baby Jesus in her arms, came down to Earth to visit a monastery.

The monks proudly lined up to pay homage to her: one recited a few poems, another showed her some beautiful illuminations for the Bible, while another recited the names of all the saints.

At the end of the line was a humble monk who hadn't had the opportunity to learn from the sages of the day.

His parents were simple folk who worked in a circus. When his turn came, the monks tried to bring the homage to a close, afraid he might bring the monastery into disrepute.

But he, too, wanted to show the Virgin his love. Under the disapproving gaze of his brothers, he shyly took some oranges from his pockets and began juggling them, as his parents had taught him at the circus.

Only then did the Baby Jesus smile and joyfully clap His hands. And it was only to him that the Virgin reached out her arms and let him hold her son for a moment.

Don't try to be consistent all the time. As Saint Paul says: "The wisdom of this world is foolishness in God's sight."

Being consistent means making sure your tie always matches your socks. It's feeling obliged to have the same opinions tomorrow that you had today. But the world is constantly changing.

As long as you don't harm anyone, then go ahead and change your opinion now and then, and contradict yourself without feeling embarrassed.

You have a right to do that. It doesn't matter what other people think, because they'll think whatever they want to.

So just relax. Let the Universe turn around you, and discover the joy of surprising yourself. "God chose what is foolish in the world to shame the wise," says Saint Paul.

MAKTUB

THE MASTER SAYS:

Today it would be good to do something out of the ordinary.

We could, for example, dance along the street on our way to work. We could look a complete stranger in the eye and speak of love at first sight. We could suggest to our boss an idea that, however ridiculous it might seem, is nevertheless one that we believe in. Or we could buy a musical instrument we always wanted to play but never dared. Warriors of light allow themselves such days.

Today we could weep over some ancient grief that still catches in our throat. We could phone someone we swore never to speak to again (but whose voice we would love to hear

PAULO COELHO

leaving a message on our voicemail). Today could be considered a day that diverges from the script we write for ourselves every morning.

Today, all mistakes will be allowed and forgiven. Today is a day for being glad to be alive.

THE SCIENTIST Roger Penrose was walking along the street with a friend, both talking animatedly. They fell silent for a moment in order to cross the road.

"I remember that, while I was crossing the road, an incredible idea occurred to me," says Penrose. "But as soon as we reached the other side and resumed our conversation, I couldn't recall what I had thought just seconds before."

Later that day, Penrose had a strange feeling of elation but couldn't figure out why.

"I had a sense that something important had been revealed to me," he says.

He went through all the things that had happened to him that day, and when he recalled the moment of silence as he crossed the road, the idea came back. This time he managed to write it down.

It was his theory regarding the existence of black holes, a real revolution in modern physics. And the idea returned to Penrose because he was able to remember the silence that always falls whenever we pause to cross a road.

Saint Anthony was living in the desert when a young man came to see him.

"Father, I have sold everything I had and given it to the poor. I kept just a few things that I would need in order to survive here in the desert. I would like you to show me the path to salvation."

Saint Anthony asked the young man to sell the few things he had kept and, with the money, buy some meat. On his way back from the town, he should tie the meat to his body.

The young man obeyed. On his return, he was attacked by dogs and by birds who all wanted a bite of that meat.

"Here I am," said the young man, revealing his torn and scratched body and clothes.

"Those who take a first step along a new path but still want to hang on to a little of their former life will end up being torn to pieces by their past," said the saint.

PAULO COELHO

THE MASTER SAYS:

Enjoy all the lovely things that God gives you today. You cannot save them up. There is no bank where you can deposit them to be used later on. If you don't use those blessings now, they will be lost forever.

God knows that we are all artists of life. One day, He gives us stones to sculpt; on another day, He gives us brushes and a canvas, or a pen to write with. But those stones are no use when it comes to painting, and the pen is useless for making sculptures.

Each day has its own miracle. Accept those blessings and create your small works of art today.

Tomorrow you will receive more blessings.

MAKTUB

THE MONASTERY ON the shores of the River Piedra is surrounded by lush greenery, a real oasis in that arid part of Spain. There, the small river becomes a rushing torrent and divides up to form dozens of waterfalls.

The traveler is walking along, listening to the music of the water. Suddenly, he notices a small grotto beneath one of the waterfalls. He studies the stone worn smooth by time, the beautiful shapes patiently created by Nature. And written on a plaque, he sees these words by Indian poet-philosopher Rabindranath Tagore, the first non-European and the first lyricist to win the Nobel Prize in Literature:

"It wasn't the sculptor's hammer that shaped these stones so perfectly. It was the water, with its gentleness, its dance, and its song. Harshness destroys; gentleness shapes."

PAULO COELHO

THE MASTER SAYS:

Many people are afraid of happiness. For them, the word means changing their habits and losing their identity.

We often believe we are unworthy of the good things that happen to us. We won't accept them because to do so would make us feel we are somehow indebted to God.

We think: "Best not drink from the cup of happiness because when it's taken away from us, we will only suffer more."

We are so afraid of being diminished that we cease to grow. We are so afraid of weeping that we stop laughing.

MAKTUB

ONE AFTERNOON IN the Scetis monastery, a monk insulted another monk. The superior, Abbot Sisois, asked the latter to forgive his aggressor.

"Certainly not," said the monk. "He must pay for what he did."

At that same moment, Abbot Sisois raised his arms to heaven and began to pray:

"Lord Jesus, we no longer need You because we ourselves can make our aggressors pay for their offenses. We can take revenge into our own hands and deal with Good and Evil too. So please, leave us to our own devices, and don't worry about us anymore."

Shamed, the monk immediately forgave his brother monk.

PAULO COELHO

"ALL THE GREAT masters say that spiritual treasure is something you can only find on your own, so why are we here together?" asked one of the disciples.

"You are together because a forest is always stronger than a single tree," said the master. "The forest retains moisture, can better withstand hurricanes, and helps to keep the soil fertile. But what makes the tree strong are its roots. And the roots of a plant cannot help another plant to grow.

"Being together with the same goal in mind and yet allowing each individual to grow in his own way, that is the path of those who wish to commune with God."

MAKTUB

WHEN THE TRAVELER was ten, his mother sent him on a physical education course.

One of the exercises involved jumping from a bridge into the water. He would always go to the end of the line, and terrified because it would soon be his turn, he would watch as each boy ahead of him jumped in. One day, his teacher—seeing how afraid he was—made him go to the front so that he would be the first to jump.

He still felt afraid, but it was over so quickly that he lost his fear.

The master says:

Often we simply have to let things take their course. At other times, though, we have to roll up our sleeves and act. Then, the worst thing you can do is to put off the moment.

PAULO COELHO

ONE MORNING, BUDDHA was gathered together with his disciples, when a man came up to him.

"Does God exist?" the man asked.

"He does," said Buddha.

After lunch, another man came over to him.

"Does God exist?" he asked.

"No, he doesn't," said Buddha.

Later that afternoon, a third man asked the same question: "Does God exist?"

"That's for you to decide," said Buddha.

"That's absurd, master," said one of his disciples. "How can you give a different answer to the same question?"

"Because each of those people is different," said Buddha. "And each will approach God in his own way, through certainty, denial, or doubt."

MAKTUB

WE ARE ALL creatures preoccupied with acting, doing, making decisions, making arrangements. We are always trying to plan something, to conclude something else, and to discover a third thing.

There's nothing wrong with that; after all, this is how we build and change the world, but the act of worship is also part of life.

Stop now and then, step outside yourself, and stand in silence before the Universe.

Kneel down with body and soul. Without asking anything, without thinking, without even feeling grateful. Simply experience the silent love wrapping around us. In such moments, a few unexpected tears—neither tears of joy nor of sorrow—might fall.

Don't be surprised. This is a gift. Those tears are washing your soul clean.

PAULO COELHO

The master says:

If you have to cry, then cry the way children cry.

You were a child once, and one of the first things you learned in life was to cry, because it's part of being alive. Never forget that you are free and that showing your emotions is nothing to be ashamed of.

Scream, sob loudly, make a noise if you want, because that is how children cry, and they know this is the most effective way of soothing their heart.

Have you noticed how children stop crying?

Something distracts them, something calls them to some new adventure.

Children stop crying very quickly.

That's how it will be for you too, but only if you cry the way a child cries.

MAKTUB

THE TRAVELER IS having lunch with a woman friend, a lawyer, in Fort Lauderdale. An overexcited drunk at the next table insists on trying to butt in on their conversation. At one point, the lawyer asks him to leave them alone, but the drunk says:

"Why? I spoke of love the way a sober man never could. I was feeling happy and wanted to communicate that happiness to two strangers. What's wrong with that?"

"It just isn't the right moment," she says.

"Do you mean there's a right moment to show that you're happy?"

They immediately invite the man to join them at their table.

THE MASTER SAYS:

We should look after our body, because it is the temple of the Holy Spirit and deserves our respect and our love.

We should make the most of our time because we must fight for our dreams and focus all our efforts on that fight.

However, it's also important to remember that life is made up of small pleasures. They were put there to provide a stimulus, to help us in our search, to give us a few moments of respite as we fight our daily battles.

It isn't a sin to be happy. There's nothing wrong, now and again, with breaking certain rules regarding diet, sleep, happiness.

Don't blame yourself if, now and then, you waste time on some silly nonsense. These are the small pleasures that provide us with the larger stimuli we need to carry on.

MAKTUB

WHILE THE MASTER was away traveling to spread the word of God, the house where he lived with his disciples caught fire.

"He entrusted us with this house, and we failed to take care of it," said one of his disciples.

They immediately started rebuilding the house from the charred remains, but the master returned sooner than expected. When he saw the work in progress, he said cheerfully:

"Gosh, a new house! We're going up in the world!"

Feeling ashamed, one of the disciples told him what really happened, that the place where they were living was destroyed by fire.

"I don't understand," said the master. "All I see are men who have faith in life and are beginning a new stage in their lives. Those who have lost the only thing they had are in a better position than many people because, from now on, they can only gain."

PAULO COELHO

THE PIANIST Arthur Rubinstein was late for lunch at a classy New York restaurant. His friends began to get worried, but finally Rubinstein appeared, arm in arm with a spectacular blonde woman thirty years his junior.

Although known for his stinginess, that afternoon he ordered the most expensive dishes and the rarest and most sophisticated wines. At the end, he paid the bill with a smile on his lips.

"I know you must be puzzled," said Rubinstein, "but today I went to see my lawyer to draw up my will. I left a nice fat sum to my daughter and to my relatives, I made generous donations to various charities, and then suddenly, I realized that *I* wasn't included in my will. All the money was going to other people!

"I decided that, from now on, I would be more generous with myself."

MAKTUB

THE MASTER SAYS:

If you are following the path of your dreams, then commit yourself to it fully. Don't leave the exit door open with the excuse "No, this isn't quite what I wanted." Those words contain the seed of defeat.

Embrace your chosen path, even if you do occasionally stumble, even if you know you could do better. If you accept what you are capable of doing now, in the present, you will be sure to improve in the future, but if you deny your limitations, you will never be free of them.

Face your journey with courage. Don't be afraid of other people's criticisms. Above all, don't let yourself be paralyzed by your own self-criticism.

God will be there with you on sleepless nights and will dry your hidden tears with His love.

God is the God of the brave.

PAULO COELHO

THE MASTER ASKED his disciples to find them all some food. They were traveling and could not cook for themselves.

The disciples returned as dusk was falling. Each of them brought what little they had managed to get from other people's charity: rotten fruit, stale bread, and sour wine.

However, one of the disciples brought a bag of ripe apples.

"I will always do whatever I can to help my master and my brothers," he said, sharing the apples.

"Where did you get these?" asked the master.

"I had to steal them," said the disciples. "The people I met only gave me stale old stuff, even though they know that we're preaching the word of God."

"Well, you can take your apples and leave and never come back," said the master. "Anyone who steals *for* me will end up stealing *from* me."

MAKTUB

WE SET OUT into the world in search of our dreams and our ideals. We often put things that are actually within easy reach in the most inaccessible of places. When we realize our mistake, we feel we have wasted our time searching in some far-off location for what was always near at hand. We blame ourselves for the mistakes we made, for having searched in vain, for the unhappiness we caused.

The master says:

Even if the treasure is buried in your own house, you will only find it when you go far away. If Peter had not experienced the pain of denying Jesus, he would not have been chosen as the father of the Church. If the prodigal son had not left everything behind him, his father would not have celebrated his return with a feast.

There are some things in our lives that bear a seal on which is written: "You will only understand my worth when, having lost me, you find me again." There is no point in trying to shorten the journey.

MAKTUB

THE MASTER MET up with his favorite disciple and asked how he was progressing in his spiritual life. The disciple responded by saying that he was managing to devote every moment of his day to God.

"Then all that's left is for you to forgive your enemies," said the master.

The disciple turned to him, shocked, and said:

"But I don't need to. I'm not angry with my enemies."

"Do you think God is angry with you?" asked the master.

"Of course not!" said the disciple.

"And yet you ask Him for His forgiveness, don't you? Well, do the same with your enemies, even if you don't hate them. By forgiving, you are washing and perfuming your own heart."

PAULO COELHO

THE YOUNG NAPOLEON was shaking like a leaf during the ferocious bombardments at the siege of Toulon.

When a soldier saw this, he said to his comrades:

"Look, he's absolutely terrified!"

"Yes," said Napoleon, "but I carry on fighting anyway. If you felt half the fear I'm feeling, you would have run away long ago."

The master says:

Fear is not a sign of cowardice. It is fear that allows us to act with courage and dignity in every situation. Anyone who feels afraid, but carries on undaunted, is proving his courage. Someone who faces dangerous situations unaware of the danger is merely acting irresponsibly.

MAKTUB

THE TRAVELER IS attending a celebration of Saint John's feast day, with stalls, shooting galleries, and homemade food.

Suddenly a clown starts imitating his every gesture. The other people laugh, and so does the traveler. In the end, he invites the clown to have a coffee with him.

"Throw yourself into life," says the clown. "If you're alive, you need to wave your arms about, hop up and down, make a noise, laugh and talk with people, because life is the exact opposite of death. Dying means staying in the same position for ever. If you're too still, you're not fully alive."

PAULO COELHO

A POWERFUL KING summoned a holy father, who was said to have healing powers, to help him with his back pain.

"God will help us," said the holy man. "But first we need to understand the reason for the pain. Confession makes us confront our problems and frees us from many things."

And the holy man began questioning the king about his life, from the way he treated his fellow man to the anxieties and difficulties of being a monarch. The king grew bored with thinking about all these problems. Turning to the holy man, he said:

"I don't want to talk about such matters. Please, bring me someone who can cure me without asking any questions."

The holy man left and returned half an hour later with another man.

"Here's the man you need," he said. "My friend is a veterinarian, and he doesn't usually talk to his patients."

MAKTUB

ONE MORNING, DISCIPLE and master were walking in the countryside.

The disciple asked his master to recommend a purifying diet, but however much the master insisted that all food is sacred, the disciple refused to believe him.

"There must be some food that will bring us closer to God," he said.

"You may be right. Those mushrooms over there, for example," said the master.

The disciple grew excited, thinking that the mushrooms would bring him purification and ecstasy. However, when he looked more closely, he screamed:

"But those are poisonous mushrooms! If I ate one of them, I would be dead within an hour!"

"Well, that's the only way I know of getting closer to God through food," said the master.

PAULO COELHO

IN THE WINTER of 1981, the traveler and his wife were walking through the streets of Prague, when they saw a young man making drawings of the buildings around him. The traveler liked one of the drawings and decided to buy it.

When he held out the money, he noticed that the young man wasn't wearing gloves, even though it was 23°F.

"Why aren't you wearing gloves?" he asked.

"So that I can hold my pencil."

They talked a little about Prague. The young man decided that he would make a sketch of the traveler's wife for free.

While he was waiting, the traveler realized that something strange had happened; they had been talking for almost five minutes even though they didn't know each other's language.

They had communicated using only gestures, smiles, and facial expressions, but the desire to share something meant that they had entered the world of language without words.

MAKTUB

A FRIEND TOOK Hassam to the door of a mosque, where a blind man was begging for alms.

"This blind man is the wisest man in the country," he said.

"How long have you been blind?" asked Hassam.

"Since birth," said the man.

"And how did you acquire so much wisdom?"

"Refusing to accept my blindness, I tried to be an astronomer," said the man. "Since I couldn't see the sky, I was obliged to imagine the stars, the sun, and all the galaxies. The closer I came to God's work, the closer I came to His wisdom."

PAULO COELHO

IN A REMOTE bar in Spain, near a town called Olite, there is a sign written by its owner:

"Just when I'd managed to find all the answers, they changed all the questions."

The master says:

We're always busily trying to find answers, and we consider answers to be important if we are to understand the meaning of life.

It's far more important to live life to the fullest and to allow time itself to reveal the meaning of life. If we try too hard to find a meaning, we're not allowing Nature to do its job, and we become incapable of reading God's signs.

THERE'S AN AUSTRALIAN story about a magus who was out walking with his three sisters when they were approached by the most famous warrior of the day.

"I want to marry one of these lovely girls," said the warrior.

"If one of them marries, the others will be sad. I'm looking for a tribe whose warriors can have three wives," said the magus, walking on.

And for years, he traveled the whole Australian continent but never found such a tribe.

"At least one of us could have been happy," said one of the sisters when they were old and weary of all that walking.

"I was wrong," said the magus, "and now it's too late."

And he turned his three sisters into blocks of stone so that those who passed by would understand that the happiness of one does not necessarily mean the unhappiness of others.

PAULO COELHO

THE JOURNALIST Wagner Carelli went to interview the Argentinean writer Jorge Luis Borges.

At the end of the interview, they continued talking about the language that exists beyond words and about the immense capacity we humans have to understand each other.

"Let me give you an example," said Borges.

And he began saying something in a strange language. When he finished, he asked Carelli if he had understood.

Before Carelli could respond, the photographer who was with him said:

"It's the Lord's Prayer."

"Exactly," said Borges. "And I was saying it in Finnish."

A CIRCUS TRAINER manages to keep an elephant captive thanks to one very simple trick: when the elephant is still a baby, the trainer ties one of its legs to a thick tree trunk.

However hard it tries, the baby elephant cannot free itself, and so gradually it becomes accustomed to the idea that the tree trunk is the stronger party.

When fully grown and endowed with enormous strength, the elephant only has to be tethered to a slender stick, and it still won't try to break free because it remembers all the times it had tried and failed.

Our legs are tethered to something equally fragile, but because, as children, we became accustomed to being tethered to a tree trunk, we don't even try to break free, unaware that it would take only one brave gesture for us to find our freedom.

PAULO COELHO

THERE'S NO POINT asking someone to explain God; they can say all the pretty words they like, but ultimately, they are merely words. Just as you could read a whole encyclopedia about love and still have no idea what it means to love someone.

The master says:

No one will ever be able to prove that God does or doesn't exist. Certain things in life are made to be experienced, not explained.

Love is one of those things. God—who *is* love—is another. Faith is a childish experience in the magical sense that Jesus taught us: "The Kingdom of God belongs to children."

God is never going to enter through your head. The door He uses is your heart.

MAKTUB

THE FATHER ABBOT used to say of Abbot João Pequeno that he prayed so much that he needn't worry about temptations anymore because he had already overcome them all.

The words of the Father Abbot finally reached the ears of one of the wise monks in the Scetis monastery, who summoned the novices to come to him after supper.

"You will have heard it said that Abbot João has no more temptations to overcome," he told them. "However, having nothing to struggle against weakens the soul. Let us pray to God to send Abbot João a really powerful temptation, and if he overcomes that temptation, let us ask God to send him another and another. And when he is once again battling against those temptations, let us pray that he will never again say: 'Lord, drive that demon away.' Let us pray that he may say instead: 'Lord, give me strength to face down evil.'"

PAULO COELHO

THERE IS A time of day, dusk, when it is hard to see clearly, when day and night meet, and nothing is totally clear or totally dark. In most spiritual traditions, this moment is considered to be sacred.

Catholic tradition teaches us that we should say the Ave Maria at six o'clock in the evening. According to a Quechua tradition, if we meet a friend in the afternoon and are still with him at dusk, we should start all over again and say, "Good evening."

At dusk, the equilibrium of the planet and of humankind is put to the test. God mixes darkness and light in order to see if the Earth has the courage to keep on turning.

If the Earth is not scared of the dark, then the night passes, and a new sun rises.

MAKTUB

The German philosopher Arthur Schopenhauer was walking along a street in Dresden, seeking answers to the questions troubling him. Suddenly, he came across a garden and decided to spend a few hours contemplating the flowers.

One of the people living close by noticed the man's strange behavior and called the police. Minutes later, a policeman went over to Schopenhauer and asked sternly:

"Who are you?"

Schopenhauer looked the man up and down and replied:

"If you could give me the answer to that question, I would be eternally grateful."

A MAN IN search of wisdom decided to go into the mountains because he had been told that, every two years, God appeared there.

For the first year, he ate everything that the Earth provided. Finally, though, the food ran out, and he had to go back to the city.

"God is most unfair!" he cried. "Didn't He see me there, waiting to hear His voice? Now I'm hungry and have to go back to the city without having heard Him."

At that moment, an angel appeared.

"God would really like to talk to you," said the angel. "He gave you food for a whole year. He was hoping that, the following year, you would provide your own food. But what did you plant? Nothing. If a man cannot produce food from the place where he lives, then he clearly isn't ready to speak to God."

MAKTUB

WE THINK: "IT really seems as if our freedom consists in choosing our own particular form of slavery. I work eight hours a day, and if I get promoted, I'll work twelve hours a day. I got married, and now I have no time for myself. I sought out God, which means I'm now obliged to attend services, masses, religious ceremonies. Everything that is important in life—love, work, faith—ends up becoming a very heavy burden."

The master says:

Only love allows us to escape. Only love for what we do with our freedom.

If we cannot love, then we might as well stop right there. Jesus said: "If your eye causes you to sin, pluck it out and cast it from you. It is better for you to enter into life with one eye, rather than have two eyes and be cast into hell fire."

Harsh words, but that's how it is.

PAULO COELHO

A HERMIT FASTED for a whole year, eating only once a week. After this great effort, he asked God to reveal to him the true meaning of a certain passage from the Bible.

He received no reply.

"What a waste of time," thought the hermit. "I made a huge sacrifice, and God doesn't even bother to answer. I'd be better off leaving this place and finding another monk who might know the meaning of that passage."

At this point, an angel appeared and said:

"Those twelve months of fasting served only to make you believe you were better than others, and God doesn't listen to vain people. But when you were humble enough to consider asking someone else for help, that's when God sent me."

And the angel revealed to the hermit what he wanted to know.

MAKTUB

73

Observe how certain words were constructed to reveal their true meaning.

Take the word "preoccupation" and divide it in two: "pre" and "occupation." It means occupying your mind or worrying about something before it actually happens.

Who, in the entire Universe, can possibly worry about something that hasn't even happened?

Discard all such preoccupations. Remain focused on your destiny and on your path. Learn everything you need to know in order to wield the sword of light that has been given to you.

Observe the fighting techniques of friends, masters, and enemies.

Train hard, but do not make that worst of all mistakes: believing that you know what your adversary's next move is going to be.

PAULO COELHO

IT'S FRIDAY, AND you arrive home and pick up the newspapers you didn't have time to read during the week. You put the TV on mute and play a CD. You use the remote control to flip from channel to channel while leafing through one of the papers and listening to the music. The newspapers tell you nothing new, the TV schedules repeat the same thing over and over, and you've heard that CD dozens of times.

Your wife is looking after the kids, sacrificing the best part of her youth without really understanding why.

An excuse comes into your head: "Well, that's what life is like." No, life isn't like that. Life is enthusiasm. Find out where you've hidden your enthusiasm. Take your wife and your kids and go after it before it's too late. Love never stopped anyone from following his dreams.

MAKTUB

ON CHRISTMAS EVE, the traveler and his wife were weighing up the year that was now coming to an end.

Over supper in the only restaurant in a village in the Pyrenees, the traveler began complaining about something that hadn't gone quite the way he wanted.

His wife was staring at the Christmas tree adorning the restaurant. The traveler assumed she wasn't interested in what he was saying and so changed the subject.

"Lovely lights," he said.

"Yes," said his wife. "But if you look closely, in the midst of all those dozens of lights, there's one that has burned out. It seems to me that instead of seeing the past year as dozens of bright lights, you can see only the one bulb that didn't light up anything."

PAULO COELHO

"YOU SEE THAT humble holy man walking down the street?" said one devil to another. "Well, I'm going to go over and win his soul."

"He won't listen because he's only interested in holy things," said his companion.

But the ever-crafty devil dressed himself up as the angel Gabriel and appeared before the man.

"I have come to help you," he said.

"I think you must be confusing me with someone else," replied the holy man. "I've never in my life done anything to deserve being visited by an angel."

And he went on his way, unaware of the danger he had avoided.

MAKTUB

JOURNALIST ÂNGELA PONTUAL went to see a show on Broadway. During intermission, she went to the bar for a whiskey. The place was packed with people smoking, talking, drinking.

A pianist was playing, but no one was paying any attention. Pontual sipped her drink and listened. The pianist looked bored, playing purely because he was being paid to do so, longing for intermission to end.

When she was on her third whiskey, she walked, slightly unsteadily, over to the pianist and bellowed:

"Are you stupid or what? Why don't you play what you want to play?"

The pianist looked at her in surprise, then almost immediately, he did start playing the music he really wanted to play. Soon a complete silence fell, and when the pianist finished, he was greeted with enthusiastic applause.

PAULO COELHO

SAINT FRANCIS OF ASSISI was a very popular young man-about-town when he decided to abandon everything and begin his work. Saint Clare of Assisi was a beautiful young woman when she took her vow of chastity. Saint Ramon Llull was among the great intellects of his day when he withdrew from the world.

The spiritual search is, above all, a challenge. Anyone who uses it in order to escape from his problems will never get very far.

There's no point in some friendless person withdrawing from the world. There's no point in taking a vow of poverty just because you're incapable of earning your own living. There's no point in being humble when, really, you're just a coward.

It's one thing to have and to renounce what you have. It's quite another not to have and to condemn those who do have.

MAKTUB

It's very easy for an impotent man to go about preaching chastity, but what value is there in that?

The master says:

Praise God's work. Learn to conquer yourself while living in the world.

HOW EASY IT is to be difficult. All you have to do is avoid other people and thus avoid pain, never running the risk of falling in love, of being disappointed, or of having your dreams crushed.

How easy it is to be difficult. You don't have to bother with phone calls that need to be made, with people asking you for help, with charitable acts you ought to perform.

How easy it is to be difficult. You just have to pretend that you live in an ivory tower and have never shed a single tear. It's enough to spend the rest of your existence playing a role.

How easy it is to be difficult. You simply have to let go of all the very best things in life.

THE PATIENT TURNED to his doctor:

"Doctor, my life is so dominated by fear that I can no longer enjoy living."

To which the doctor replied:

"There's a mouse in my consulting room who is gnawing away at my books. If I get really worked up about this mouse, he'll hide away from me, and I'll waste all my time hunting him. So, I have put my most important books away in a safe place, leaving him to gnaw at the others. That way, he continues to be a mouse and doesn't turn into a monster. Be afraid of some things and focus your fear on those, so that you can be brave about everything else."

PAULO COELHO

THE MASTER SAYS:

It's often easier to love than to be loved.

We find it hard to accept the help and support of others. However, our attempt to appear independent means that someone else misses out on an opportunity to show us his or her love.

Many parents, in old age, don't give their children the chance to offer them the same love and support they received when they were young. When one of fate's lightning bolts strikes them down, many husbands or wives feel ashamed at having to depend on their spouse. This stops the waters of love from spreading.

We need to accept the loving gesture offered by our fellow

MAKTUB

human beings. We need to allow others to help us, to support us, and to give us strength to carry on.

If we accept this love openly and humbly, we will come to understand that love isn't a question of giving or receiving but of sharing.

PAULO COELHO

EVE WAS STROLLING in the Garden of Eden when the serpent came over to her.

"Eat this apple," he said.

Eve, who had been well trained by God, refused.

"Eat this apple," said the serpent again, "because you need to look as beautiful as you can for your man."

"No, I don't," answered Eve, "because he has no other woman but me."

The serpent laughed.

"Oh yes he does."

And when Eve wouldn't believe him, he led her to the top of a hill where there was a well.

"She's inside this cave. Adam hid her there."

Eve leaned over and saw a lovely woman reflected in the water of the well. She didn't hesitate then, and ate the apple the serpent was offering her.

MAKTUB

FRAGMENTS FROM AN anonymous "letter to my heart":

"Dear heart, I will never condemn you, criticize you, or feel ashamed of your words. I know that you are one of God's beloved children and that He keeps you wrapped in a loving, radiant light.

"I trust you, dear heart. I am on your side, and in my prayers, I will always ask for blessings to rain down on you and for you always to find the help and support that you need.

"I trust in your love, dear heart. I trust that you will share that love with those who deserve or need it. Let my path be your path, and let us walk together toward the Holy Spirit.

PAULO COELHO

"And I ask you: please trust in me. Know that I love you and that I am trying to give you the freedom you need if you are to continue beating joyfully in my breast. I will do everything I can to make sure that my presence around you is never bothersome."

MAKTUB

THE MASTER SAYS:

When we decide to act, it's only natural that unexpected conflicts will arise. It's also natural that we might get hurt.

Wounds heal, and scars remain, but they are a blessing. Those scars will stay with us for the rest of our lives and will be of great help to us. If, at some point—for whatever reason, selfish or otherwise—the pull to return to the past proves very strong, we only have to look at those scars.

The scars will show us the marks left by handcuffs, they will remind us of the horrors of prison, and then we will keep walking straight ahead.

PAULO COELHO

IN HIS EPISTLE to the Corinthians, Saint Paul tells us that kindness is one of the main characteristics of love.

We must never forget that love is kind. A very rigid soul will not allow the hand of God to mold it according to His desires.

The traveler was walking along a narrow path in the north of Spain when he came upon a local man lying in a garden.

"Are you picking flowers?" he asked.

"No," the man replied. "I'm trying to soak up a little of their kindness."

MAKTUB

THE MASTER SAYS:

Pray every day. Even if you use no words, make no requests, have no idea why you're praying, make prayer a habit. If this seems hard at first, say to yourself: "This week, I am going to pray every day." Renew that promise every seven days.

Remember that you are not only forging a closer link with the spiritual world but also training your will. It is through such practices that we develop the discipline needed for the real battle of life.

There's no point in forgetting your promise and praying twice the next day. Nor is there any point in praying seven times on one day and spending the rest of the week thinking that you have fulfilled your task.

Some things need to happen at a certain pace and rhythm.

PAULO COELHO

A BAD MAN dies and meets an angel at the gates of hell.

The angel says to him:

"You only have to have done one good thing in this life, and that good thing will save you."

The man answers:

"I've never done anything good."

"Think hard," says the angel.

The man remembers then that once, while walking in a forest, he had seen a spider on the path ahead and had deliberately walked around it to avoid crushing it.

The angel smiles, and a spider's thread descends from the heavens, allowing the man to climb up to Paradise. However, when other condemned men try to climb up behind him, he turns and starts pushing them back, afraid the thread will break.

MAKTUB

At that moment, the thread does break, and the man plummets back into hell.

"What a shame," he hears the angel say. "Your selfishness transformed the one good thing you ever did into something bad."

THE MASTER SAYS:

Crossroads are sacred places. That is where the pilgrim must make a decision. This is why the gods tend to sleep and eat at crossroads.

Wherever paths cross, two powerful energies coalesce—the path that will be chosen and the path that will be abandoned. Both become a single path, but only for a very brief period of time.

The pilgrim can rest and sleep a little, or even consult the gods who inhabit the crossroads. But no one can stay there forever; once his choice has been made, the pilgrim must carry on and never think about the path not taken.

If he does, the crossroads become a curse.

MAKTUB

THE HUMAN RACE has committed its worst crimes in the name of Truth. Men and women were burned. Entire civilizations were destroyed.

Those who committed sins of the flesh were cast out. Those who sought a different path were marginalized.

One of them was crucified in the name of the "truth," but before he died, he left a magnificent definition of Truth.

It isn't what gives us certainties.

It isn't what gives us profound thoughts.

It isn't what makes us better than others.

It isn't what keeps us locked inside the prison of our prejudices.

The Truth is what makes us free.

"Know the Truth," He said, "and the Truth will make you free."

PAULO COELHO

ONE OF THE monks from the Scetis monastery committed a very grave fault, and the wisest of the hermits was summoned to pass judgment on him.

The hermit refused to come, but the other monks were so insistent that, in the end, he did. First, though, he took a bucket and made several holes in it. Then he filled it with sand and walked to the monastery.

When the Father Superior saw him, he asked about the bucket.

"I came to judge my fellow man," said the hermit. "My sins are spilling out behind me just as the sand is spilling out of this bucket. But since I do not look back and cannot see my own sins, I have been summoned to judge my fellow man!"

The monks immediately decided not to proceed with any punishment.

MAKTUB

WRITTEN ON THE wall of a small church in the Pyrenees:

Lord, may this candle be a light to illumine all my decisions and difficulties.

Let it be a fire so that You can burn up inside me all egotism, pride, and impurity.

May it be a flame so that You can warm my heart and teach me how to love.

I cannot stay for very long in Your church, but by leaving this candle, a small part of me will remain here and help me prolong my prayer in all that I do today. Amen.

PAULO COELHO

A FRIEND OF the traveler decided to spend a few weeks in a monastery in Nepal. One afternoon, he went into one of the monastery's many temples and found a monk sitting on the altar, smiling.

"Why are you smiling?" he asked the monk.

"Because I have just understood the meaning of bananas," said the monk, opening the bag he was holding and taking out a rotten banana. "This is the life that has passed and that we failed to enjoy to the fullest at the time, and now it is too late."

Then he took from his bag a banana that was still very green.

He held it up, then put it away again.

"This is the life that has not yet happened and must await its moment," he said.

Finally, he brought out a perfectly ripe banana, peeled it, and shared it with the traveler's friend, saying:

"This is the present moment. Learn to live it without fear."

MAKTUB

BABY CONSUELO HAD set off with just the right amount of money to pay for her and her son to go to the movies.

The boy was very excited and kept asking if they were there yet.

When they drew up at a red light, she saw a beggar sitting on the pavement, except that he wasn't begging. She heard a voice say:

"Give him all the money you have with you."

Baby argued with the voice; she had, after all, promised to take her son to the movies.

"Give it to him," said the voice.

"I can give him half, then my son can see the movie on his own, and I'll wait outside," she said.

But the voice was in no mood to argue.

"Give it all to him."

Baby didn't have time to explain to her son what she was

doing. She stopped the car and handed all the money she had to the beggar.

"God must exist, and you are the proof of that," said the beggar. "Today is my birthday. I was feeling sad and ashamed still to be begging. So, I decided not to beg today, thinking: if God exists, he will give me a present."

MAKTUB

A PILGRIM IS walking through a village in the middle of a storm, and he sees a house on fire.

As he gets nearer, he can make out a man still sitting in his burning living room, up to his eyes in flames.

"Hey, your house is on fire!" shouts the pilgrim.

"I know," says the man.

"So why don't you leave?"

"Because it's raining," says the man. "And my mother told me that if you get caught in the rain, you might get pneumonia."

Zao Chi comments:

"Wise is the man who knows how to change his situation when he has to."

PAULO COELHO

IN SOME MAGIC traditions, the disciples spend one day a year—or a weekend if necessary—making contact with all the objects in their house.

They touch each thing and ask out loud:

"Do I really need this?"

They take the books from the shelf.

"Will I ever read this again?"

They look at the various souvenirs they have kept.

"Do I still consider the moment this reminds me of to be important?"

They open their wardrobes.

"I've had this for ages and never worn it. Do I really need it?"

The master says:

Things have their own energy. When they're not used, they become like stagnant water, a good place for mosquitoes and decay.

You need to remain alert and allow energy to flow freely. If you hang on to what is old, the new has no place in which to reveal itself.

An old Peruvian legend tells of a city where everyone was happy. Its inhabitants did what they liked and got on well with each other—everyone, that is, except the governor, who was miserable because he had no governing to do.

The prison was empty, the court was never used, and the notary's office made no money because a person's word was worth more than a piece of paper.

One day, the prefect summoned some workmen from outside the city, and they shut themselves up behind a screen in the middle of the main square, where all that could be heard was the sound of hammering and sawing.

A week later, the governor invited all the citizens to the inauguration. The screen was ceremoniously removed to reveal . . . a gallows.

People asked what such a thing was doing there. Filled with uncertainty and fear, they began going to the courts for

---

MAKTUB

something that, before, would have been resolved by common agreement. They went to the notary's office to register documents when, before, their word had been enough. And suspicious of the law, they once again listened to what the governor had to say.

The legend says that the gallows was never used, but its presence was enough to change everything.

THE AUSTRIAN PSYCHIATRIST Viktor Frankl describes his experience in a Nazi concentration camp and how, in the midst of all the humiliation, a fellow prisoner suddenly whispered to him: "'If our wives could see us now!' . . . That brought thoughts of my own wife to mind . . . and as we stumbled on for miles, slipping on icy spots, supporting each other time and again, dragging one another up and onward, nothing was said, but we both knew: each of us was thinking of his wife. . . .

"Then I grasped the meaning of the greatest secret that human poetry and human thought have to impart: *The salvation of man is through love and in love.* I understood how a man who has nothing left in this world still may know bliss, be it only for a brief moment, in the contemplation of his beloved. In a position of utter desolation, when man cannot express himself in positive action, when his only achievement may consist in enduring his sufferings in the right way—an

---

MAKTUB

honorable way—in such a position man can, through loving contemplation of the image he carries of his beloved, achieve fulfillment . . .

"I did not know whether my wife was alive, and I had no means of finding out . . . but at that moment, it ceased to matter. There was no need for me to know; nothing could touch the strength of my love, my thoughts, and the image of my beloved. Had I known then that my wife was dead, I think that I would still have given myself, undisturbed by that knowledge, to the contemplation of her image, and that my mental conversation with her would have been just as vivid and just as satisfying. 'Set me like a seal upon thy heart, love is as strong as death.'"

PAULO COELHO

THE MASTER SAYS:

From now on—and for the next few hundred years—the Universe is going to boycott all those who hold preconceived ideas.

Earth's energy needs to be renewed. New ideas need space. Body and soul need new challenges. The future is knocking at our door, and all ideas—apart from those based on pure prejudice—will be allowed in.

Whatever is important will remain, and whatever is useless will vanish, but we must each judge only our own successes, not the dreams of our fellow humans.

In order to have faith in our own path, we do not need to prove that another person's path is wrong. Anyone who does so clearly has no confidence in his own steps.

MAKTUB

LIFE IS LIKE a long bicycle race whose goal is the fulfillment of our Personal Legend.

At the start, we are all together, sharing comradeship and enthusiasm. As the race proceeds, though, that initial excitement gives way to the real challenges: tiredness, boredom, self-doubt. We notice that some of our friends have given up; they're still cycling, but only because they can't just stop in the middle of the road. Many of them are pedaling along beside the support van, chatting to each other and simply going through the motions.

We end up losing sight of them, and then we are obliged to face the loneliness and the surprises that are waiting around every unfamiliar bend, not to mention problems with our bike.

We end up asking if it's worth all that effort.

Yes, it is. Just don't give up.

PAULO COELHO

Master and disciple are traveling through the deserts of Arabia. The master makes the most of each moment of their journey to teach his disciple about faith.

"Entrust everything to God," he says. "God never abandons His children."

At night, when they set up camp, the master asks the disciple to tether the horses to a nearby rock. The disciple goes over to the rock, then remembers his master's teachings. "He's testing me," he thinks. "I must entrust the horses to God." And he leaves the horses untethered.

In the morning, he discovers that the horses have run away. Furious, he goes over to his master.

"You don't know anything about God," he says. "I handed the horses over to His care, and they've run away."

"God wanted to look after the horses," says the master. "But to do so, He needed your hands to tether them safely to the rock."

MAKTUB

"**Perhaps God has** sent some of His apostles down into the inferno to save souls," says John. "All is not lost, not even there."

This idea surprises the traveler. John is a fireman in Los Angeles, and this is his day off.

"Why do you say that?" the traveler asks.

"Because I know what the inferno is like. I've experienced it here on Earth. I go into burning buildings, I see desperate people trying to escape, and often I have to risk my own life to save them. I am just a tiny particle in this vast Universe, forced to behave like a hero in the midst of the many infernos I meet. If I—who am nothing—can do that, imagine what Jesus must be able to do! I'm sure that some of His apostles are down there in hell, saving souls."

THE MASTER SAYS:

The custom among many primitive civilizations was to bury the dead in the fetal position. "They are being born into another life, and so we place them in the same position they were in when they came into this world," they said. For those civilizations—in constant contact with the miracle of transformation—death was only one more step along the Universe's long road.

The world gradually lost that gentle vision of death, but it doesn't matter what we think or do or what we believe: we will all die one day.

It's best to adopt the attitude of the old Yaqui Indians: use death as a counselor and keep asking, "Given that I am going to die, what should I do now?"

MAKTUB

Life isn't a matter of asking for or giving advice. If we need help, it's best to see how other people resolve or fail to resolve their problems.

Our angel is always present and often supplies the answer in words spoken by someone else, and that answer usually comes by chance when, however preoccupied we are, we are still not allowing our own concerns to cloud the miracle of life.

Let us leave our angel to speak in the way to which he is accustomed—when he deems it necessary.

The master says:

Advice is the theory of life, but the practice tends to be very different.

PAULO COELHO

ONE DAY, A priest belonging to the Charismatic Renewal church in Rio de Janeiro was on a bus when he heard a voice telling him to stand up and preach the word of Christ right there and then. He said to the voice:

"They'll think I'm ridiculous. This is no place for a sermon."

But something inside him kept insisting that he speak.

"Look, I'm really shy. Please don't ask me to do this," he pleaded.

The inner voice persisted.

Then he remembered the promise he had made: to accept whatever Christ asked of him. Standing up—feeling horribly embarrassed—he began to talk about the Gospel. The other

MAKTUB

passengers listened in silence. He looked at each individual, and they rarely looked away. He said everything that was in his heart, then, his sermon over, he sat down.

He still doesn't know what task he was fulfilling at that moment, but he is absolutely certain that he did fulfill a task.

PAULO COELHO

AN AFRICAN WITCH doctor is leading his apprentice through the forest. Even though he is older, he walks along very nimbly, while his apprentice keeps slipping and falling over. The apprentice curses, gets up, spits on the treacherous earth, and continues to follow his master.

After a long trek, they reach a sacred place. Without even stopping, the witch doctor immediately turns around and starts walking back.

"You haven't taught me anything today," says the apprentice when he falls over yet again.

"I have, but you, it seems, have failed to learn," says the witch doctor. "I'm trying to teach you how to deal with the mistakes you make in life."

"And how should I deal with them?"

"Just as you should each time you fall," says the witch doctor. "Instead of cursing the place where you fell, you should look to see what it was that made you fall."

MAKTUB

ONE EVENING, THE Father Abbot was visiting the Scetis monastery when a hermit came to see him.

"My spiritual adviser doesn't know how to guide me," said the hermit. "Should I leave him?"

The Father Abbot said nothing, and the hermit returned to the desert. A week later, he visited the Father Abbot again.

"My spiritual adviser doesn't know how to guide me," he said again. "I have decided to leave him."

"Those are wise words," said the Father Abbot. "When a man sees that his soul is not content, then he does not ask for advice. He takes the necessary decisions to preserve his journey through this life."

PAULO COELHO

A YOUNG WOMAN goes over to the traveler and says:

"I want to tell you something. I have always believed that I have the power to heal, but I've never had the courage to try. Then, one day, my husband had a terrible pain in his left leg, and since there was no one around to help, I decided—feeling extremely embarrassed—to place my hands on his leg and pray for the pain to go away.

"I did this without actually believing that I would be able to help him, but then I heard him praying: 'Lord, let my wife be the messenger of Your light and Your strength.' My hands began to grow warm, and the pain quickly passed.

"Then I asked my husband why he had prayed like that. To give me confidence, he said. Now, thanks to those words, I can heal."

MAKTUB

The philosopher Aristippus was courting the favor of Dionysius I, the tyrant of Syracuse.

One evening, he found Diogenes preparing a small dish of lentils for himself.

"If you were to bow down to Dionysius, you wouldn't have to eat lentils," said Aristippus.

"If you could bring yourself to eat lentils, you wouldn't have to bow down to Dionysius," retorted Diogenes.

The master says:

While it's true that everything has a price, that price is relative. When we follow our dreams, we can sometimes give others the impression that we are poor, unhappy wretches, but it doesn't matter what other people think; what matters is the joy in our heart.

PAULO COELHO

A MAN LIVING in Turkey heard tell of a great master who lived in Persia.

He didn't hesitate; he sold all his belongings, said good-bye to his family, and went in search of wisdom.

After years of traveling, he finally arrived at the cabin where the great master lived. Full of fear and respect, he went over and knocked.

The great master opened the door.

"I have come all the way from Turkey," said the man. "I made the whole journey in order to ask just one question."

The old man looked at him in surprise:

"All right. You can ask just one question."

"I need to be quite clear about what I'm about to ask. May I ask it in Turkish?"

MAKTUB

119

"You may," said the master, "and I have now answered your one question. If there's anything else you want to know, then consult your heart, and it will give you the answer."

And with that he closed the door.

THE MASTER SAYS:

The word is power. Words transform the world and humankind.

We have all been told: "Don't talk about the good things in your life because other people's envy will destroy your happiness."

Not at all; life's winners speak with pride of the miracles in their lives. If you send positive energy out into the air, it will attract more positive energy and will bring joy to those who truly love you.

As for the envious, the defeated, they can only harm you if you let them.

Don't be afraid. Speak about the good things in your life with those who want to hear. The Soul of the World has great need of your joy.

MAKTUB

ONCE THERE WAS a king of Spain who took great pride in his lineage and who was known for being cruel to the weak. One day, he was traveling with his entourage through a field in Aragon where—years before—his father had lost a battle.

There he met a holy man rummaging around in a huge pile of bones.

"What are you doing there?" asked the king.

"All honor to Your Majesty," said the holy man. "When I heard that the king of Spain was coming here, I decided to find your father's bones and give them to you, but however hard I look, I cannot find them. They're exactly the same as the bones of the peasants, the poor, the beggars, and the slaves."

PAULO COELHO

"The Negro Speaks of Rivers" by Langston Hughes:

I've known rivers:

I've known rivers ancient as the world and older than the
flow of human blood in human veins.

My soul has grown deep like the rivers.

I bathed in the Euphrates when dawns were young.
I built my hut near the Congo and it lulled me to sleep.
I looked upon the Nile and raised the pyramids above it.
I heard the singing of the Mississippi when Abe Lincoln
went down to New Orleans, and I've seen its muddy
bosom turn all golden in the sunset.

I've known rivers:
Ancient, dusky rivers.

My soul has grown deep like the rivers.

MAKTUB

"**WHAT QUALITIES MAKE** the best swordsman?" asked the warrior.

"Go to the field near the monastery," said the master. "There you will find a rock. Insult it."

"Why should I do that?" asked the disciple. "The rock won't answer me back."

"Then attack it with your sword," said the master.

"I won't do that either," said the disciple. "My sword will break. And if I attack it with my bare hands, I'll hurt my fingers, and all for nothing. My question was: What qualities make the best swordsman?"

"The best swordsman is the one who most resembles that rock," said the master. "Without even unsheathing its sword, it manages to show that no one can defeat it."

PAULO COELHO

THE TRAVELER ARRIVES at the tiny hamlet of San Martín de Unx in Navarra, Spain, and manages to find the woman who keeps the key to the beautiful Romanesque church in that near ruin of a village. She very kindly leads him up the narrow alleyways and opens the door to the church.

The traveler finds the darkness and the silence of that medieval temple deeply moving. He talks a little with the woman and, at one point, comments that, even though it's midday, they can barely see the beautiful works of art inside.

"We can only see the details in the dawn light," says the woman. "According to the legend, this is what the builders of this church wanted to teach us, that God only shows us His glory at the appointed hour."

THE MASTER SAYS:

There are two gods. The god about whom our teachers taught us and the God who teaches us. The god people usually talk about and the God who talks to us. The god we learn to fear and the God who speaks to us of mercy.

There are two gods. The god who lives on high, and the God who takes part in our daily lives. The god who demands payment from us and the God who forgives us our debts. The god who threatens us with the fires of hell and the God who shows us the best path to take.

There are two gods. The god who crushes us with our many faults, and the God who sets us free with His love.

PAULO COELHO

Someone once asked Michelangelo how he was able to create such magnificent works of art.

"It's very simple," said Michelangelo. "The sculpture is already complete within the marble block before I start my work. It is already there, I just have to chisel away the superfluous material."

The master says:

There is a work of art we were all destined to create.

It is the central point of our life, and however hard we try to deny it, we know how important it is for our happiness. Usually, this work of art is covered up by years of fear, guilt, and indecision.

But if we decide to chisel away the superfluous matter, if we do not doubt our ability, we can fulfill the mission we were given. This is the only way to live with honor.

MAKTUB

AN OLD MAN who is close to death seeks out a young man and tells him a tale of heroism, of how, during a war, he helped a man to escape.

He gave him shelter, food, and protection. When they were once more in a place of safety, the man he had rescued betrayed him and handed him over to the enemy.

"But how did you escape?" asks the young man.

"I didn't. I was the other man, the traitor," says the old man. "But in telling the story as if I were the hero, I can better understand all that he did for me."

PAULO COELHO

THE MASTER SAYS:

We all need love. Love is part of human nature, as much as eating, drinking, and sleeping. We often sit watching a beautiful sunset, completely alone, and we think:

"None of this is of any importance, because I have no one with whom I can share all this beauty."

At such times, it is worth asking: How often did I turn away when another person asked for my love? How often was I afraid to approach someone and say, outright, that I was in love with them?

Beware of solitude. It is as addictive as the most dangerous of drugs. If the sunset no longer seems to have any meaning for you, then be humble and go in search of love. Remember that, as with other spiritual blessings, the more you are prepared to give, the more you will receive in exchange.

MAKTUB

A SPANISH MISSIONARY was visiting an island when he came across three Aztec priests.

"How do you pray?" asked the priest.

"We only have one prayer," said one of the Aztecs. "We say: 'God, you are three and we are three. Have mercy on us.'"

"I am going to teach you a prayer that God will hear," said the missionary.

He taught them a Catholic prayer and continued on his way.

Shortly before returning to Spain, he had to pass close by the same island he had visited a few years before.

As the ship was approaching the shore, the missionary saw the three priests walking on the waters.

PAULO COELHO

"Father, Father," said one of them. "Please teach us again the prayer that God will hear, because we can't remember it."

"No matter," said the missionary on seeing this miracle.

And he asked God's forgiveness for having failed to understand that He speaks all languages.

MAKTUB

SAINT JOHN OF THE CROSS teaches that, on our spiritual journey, we should not hope for visions or blindly follow the words of others who traveled that same road. Our one source of support should be faith, because faith is something limpid and transparent that is born inside us and cannot be confused with anything else.

A writer was talking to a priest, and he asked him what it meant to experience God.

"I don't know," said the priest. "Up until now, I have only experienced my own faith in God."

And that is what matters.

PAULO COELHO

THE MASTER SAYS:

Forgiveness is a two-way street.

Whenever we forgive someone, we are also forgiving our-selves. If we are tolerant with others, it is easier to accept our own faults. Thus, without guilt or bitterness, we can improve our attitude to life.

When, in a moment of weakness, we allow hatred, envy, and intolerance to vibrate in the air around us, those vibrations end up consuming us.

Peter asked Christ:

"Lord, how many times shall I forgive my brother or sister who sins against me? Up to seven times?"

Jesus answered, "I tell you, not seven times, but seventy-seven times."

The act of forgiveness cleanses the astral plane and shows us the true light of the Divinity.

MAKTUB

THE MASTER SAYS:

The masters of old used to create "characters" to help their disciples deal with the darker side of their personality. Many stories about the creation of such characters later became famous fairy tales.

The process is a simple one: you just have to place all your anxieties, fears, and disappointments in an invisible being who stands on your left side. He acts as the "villain" in your life, always suggesting ideas you would prefer not to have, but end up having. Once you have created such a character, it becomes easier to ignore his advice.

This is extremely simple, which is why it works so well.

PAULO COELHO

"How can I know how best to live my life?" asked the disciple.

The master asked him to make a table. When the table was almost ready—needing just a few more nails to be hammered in—the master went over to him.

The disciple was nailing in each nail with three very precise blows.

One nail, though, proved more difficult, and the disciple had to deliver an extra blow. That fourth blow drove the nail in too deeply, and the wood split.

"Your hand was used to delivering just three blows," said the master. "When any action becomes ruled by habit, it loses its meaning and can even cause harm.

"An action is just an action, and there is only one secret: never allow habit to control your movements."

MAKTUB

NEAR THE TOWN of Soria in Spain, there is an ancient hermitage in a cave where a man has been living for a few years now, a man who abandoned everything to devote himself to contemplation. One fall afternoon, the traveler goes to visit him and is welcomed most hospitably.

After sharing some bread, the hermit asks the traveler to go with him to a nearby stream to pick a few mushrooms.

On the way there, a young man approaches.

"Holy father," he says, "I have heard it said that, in order to achieve enlightenment, we shouldn't eat meat. Is that true?"

"Joyfully accept all that life offers you," says the man. "That way you will neither be committing a sin against your spirit nor will you be blaspheming against the generosity of the Earth."

THE MASTER SAYS:

If the journey proves very hard, be sure to listen to your heart. Try to be as honest as possible with yourself, and see if you really are following your path and paying the price for your dreams.

If you do this, but your life continues to be hard, there comes a moment when you must complain. Do so as respectfully as a child would to his father, but nonetheless demand a little more care and help. God is both father and mother, and parents always want the best for their children. Perhaps they're making you study too hard, and if so, there's nothing wrong with asking for a slight pause and a little affection.

But don't go too far. Job complained when it was the right moment, and all his goods were returned to him. Al Afid used to complain about everything, and God stopped listening to him.

THE FIESTAS IN the Spanish city of Valencia involve a strange ritual that has its origin in the ancient company of carpenters.

Artisans and artists work all year to construct huge wooden sculptures. In the week of the fiesta, they carry these sculptures down to the main square. People walk past, pausing to make comments, amazed and even moved by such creativity. Then, on Saint Joseph's Day, all but one of these works of art are burned on a gigantic bonfire before thousands of onlookers.

"Why all that hard work for nothing?" asked an English woman, watching the flames reaching up into the sky.

"You'll die one day too," said a Spanish woman. "Imagine if, at that moment, some angel were to ask God: 'Why all that hard work for nothing?'"

PAULO COELHO

A VERY DEVOUT and pious man suddenly found himself stripped of all his wealth. Knowing that God would help him regardless, he began to pray:

"Lord, make me win the lottery."

He repeated the same prayer for years and years and yet continued to live in poverty.

The day of his death finally arrived, and since he was a very devout man, he went straight to heaven.

When he got there, though, he refused to go in. He said he had lived his entire life in accordance with the religious precepts he had been taught, and yet God had never let him win the lottery.

"All the Lord's promises are nothing but lies," said the man angrily.

"I was always ready to help you win," said the Lord. "But however willing I was to help you, you never once bought a lottery ticket."

MAKTUB

A WISE OLD Chinese man was walking across a snowy field when he came upon a woman crying.

"Why are you crying?" he asked.

"Because I keep remembering the past, my youth, my beautiful face reflected in the mirror, the men I loved. God was cruel because he gave me a memory. He knew that I would recall the springtime of my life and weep."

The wise man stood contemplating the snowy field, his eyes fixed on a certain point. The woman eventually stopped crying and asked:

"What are you looking at?"

"A field of roses," said the wise man. "God very generously gave me a memory too. He knew that, in winter, I would always be able to remember the spring and smile."

PAULO COELHO

THE MASTER SAYS:

Following one's Personal Legend is not as simple as it seems. On the contrary, doing so can bring dangers.

When we want something, we set in motion certain very powerful energies and can no longer conceal from ourselves the true meaning of our life.

When we want something, we choose the price we will have to pay.

Following a dream has its price. It might require us to abandon old habits; it might bring with it difficulties, disappointments, etc.

However high the price, though, it is never as high as the price paid by someone who does not follow their Personal Legend, because when they look back one day, they will see everything they did and hear their own heart say: "I wasted my life."

Believe me, those are some of the cruelest words anyone can hear.

MAKTUB

IN ONE OF his books, Carlos Castañeda describes how, one day, his teacher told him to wear the belt on his pants the other way round. Castañeda did as instructed, convinced that he was being given a powerful learning tool.

Months later, he told his teacher that, thanks to this magical practice, he was learning more quickly than before.

"By wearing my belt the other way round, I have transformed negative energy into positive," he said.

The teacher burst out laughing.

"A belt can't transform energy! The reason I told you to do that was so that, whenever you put your pants on, you would remember that you are a sorcerer's apprentice. It was that awareness, not your belt, that helped you grow."

PAULO COELHO

A MASTER HAD hundreds of disciples. They all prayed at the right time except one, who was always drunk.

On the day of his death, the master summoned the drunk and revealed to him all the hidden secrets.

The other disciples were furious.

"That's disgraceful!" they cried. "We have sacrificed ourselves for a master who is incapable of seeing our qualities."

The master said:

"I needed to pass those secrets on to a man I knew well. Those who appear to be virtuous are usually concealing vanity, pride, and intolerance. That is why I chose the one disciple whose defect was plain to see: drunkenness."

MAKTUB

WORDS FROM THE Cistercian monk Marcos García:

"God sometimes withdraws a particular blessing so that the person can see Him as more than just a granter of favors and requests. He knows how far He can go in testing a soul, and He never goes beyond that point.

"At such moments, we should never say: 'God has abandoned me.' He never does that: we are the ones who can, sometimes, abandon Him. If the Lord puts us to a great test, He also always gives us enough—I would say more than enough—of the qualities needed to survive it.

"Whenever we feel far from His face, we should ask ourselves: Are we making the most of what He has placed in our path?"

PAULO COELHO

WE SOMETIMES SPEND days or whole weeks without receiving a single kind gesture from our fellow humans. These are difficult times, when human warmth vanishes, and life becomes a mere question of survival.

The master says:

We should look at our own fire. We should put on more wood and try to bring light to the dark room our life has become. When we hear our fire crackling, the wood cracking, and the many stories told by the flames, hope will be returned to us.

If we are capable of loving, we will also be capable of being loved. It's simply a matter of time.

MAKTUB

DURING SUPPER, SOMEONE broke a glass.

"That's a sign of good luck," the guest said.

Everyone there knew this tradition.

"Why is it a sign of good luck?" asked a rabbi who was part of the group.

"I don't know," said the traveler's wife. "Perhaps it's just an old way of making the guest feel at ease."

"No, that's not the right explanation," said the rabbi. "According to certain Jewish traditions, we are each given a certain quota of luck, which we use up throughout our life. If we use that luck only on things we really need, then we can earn interest, or we can just fritter it away.

"We Jews also say 'good luck' when someone breaks a glass, but what this means is that you didn't squander your luck by trying to avoid the glass breaking, and so you still have luck to use on more important things."

PAULO COELHO

ABBOT ABRAHAM KNEW that near the Scetis monastery lived a hermit who had a reputation as a sage.

He went to visit him and asked:

"If today you found a beautiful woman in your bed, would you be capable of thinking that she wasn't a woman?"

"No," said the hermit, "but I would be able to control myself."

The abbot went on:

"And if you found gold coins in the desert, would you be capable of seeing them as merely stones?"

"No," said the hermit, "but I would stop myself from picking them up."

Then Abbot Abraham asked:

"And if you were visited by two brothers, one who hated you and the other who loved you, would you be capable of treating them equally?"

The hermit answered:

"However painful, I would treat the one who loved me the same as the one who hated me."

When he returned to the monastery, the abbot said to his novices:

"I'm going to explain to you what it means to be a sage. He is someone who, instead of extinguishing his passions, manages to control them."

W. Frasier spent his whole life writing about the conquest of the American West. Proud of being able to include on his résumé the script for a movie starring Gary Cooper, he said that he had very rarely felt bored.

"I learned a lot from the American pioneers. They fought with the Indians, crossed deserts, went looking for food and water in remote regions. And all the contemporary records show one curious characteristic: the pioneers only wrote or talked about good things. Instead of complaining, they composed songs and made jokes about the difficulties they encountered. This is how they kept despair and depression at bay. And today, at the age of eighty-eight, I try to do the same."

THIS TEXT IS adapted from the words of John Muir:

I want to leave my soul free so that it may be granted all the attributes generally bestowed on spirits.

Were such a thing possible, I would not attempt to visit the craters of the moon or follow the sunbeams to their sources in the sun. I would not try to understand the beauty of our own good star or the artificial desolation of human beings.

When I have learned how to free my soul, I will follow the dawn light and seek to follow it back through time.

When I have learned how to free my soul, I will plunge into the magnetic currents that flow out into an ocean where all the waters intermingle to form the Soul of the World.

When I have learned how to free my soul, I will try to read the whole splendid page of Creation from the very beginning.

PAULO COELHO

ONE OF THE sacred symbols of Christianity is the image of the pelican. The explanation is simple: when there was no other food, the mother pelican was said to peck at her own breast and feed her chicks with her blood and flesh.

The master says:

We are often incapable of understanding the blessings we receive. We often do not understand all that God does to keep us spiritually nourished.

There is a story about a pelican who, during a very harsh winter, managed to survive her own act of self-sacrifice—feeding her chicks with her own flesh—but only for a few days. When she herself died from a lack of nourishment, one of her chicks said to the other one:

"Good. I was getting tired of eating the same thing every day."

IF YOU FEEL dissatisfied with something—even if it's something good that you would like to succeed in but have so far failed—then stop, now.

If things aren't working, there are just two possible explanations: either your powers of perseverance are being tested or you need to change direction.

To find out which of these options is the right one—given that they represent two opposing positions—seek refuge in silence and prayer. Gradually, mysteriously, things will become clear, and eventually you will have sufficient strength to make a choice.

Once you have decided, forget all about the other possibility, and move on, because God is the God of the valiant.

Domingos Sabino, father of the Brazilian author Fernando Sabino, often said to his son:

"Everything always turns out well in the end. If things aren't going well, that's because you haven't yet reached the end."

PAULO COELHO

WHEN THE COMPOSER Nelson Motta was in Bahia, Brazil, he decided to visit spiritual leader Mãe Menininha do Gantois. He took a taxi, but on the way there, the car's brakes failed, and it spun out of control in the middle of the fast lane. Apart from the shock, though, both driver and passenger were fine.

When Nelson met Mãe Menininha, he immediately told her about the accident. She said:

"There are certain things that are written in our fate, but God somehow manages to get us through them safely. A car accident at this time of your life was clearly there in your destiny, but as you see, everything happened and nothing happened."

MAKTUB

"THERE WAS SOMETHING missing from your talk about the Camino de Santiago," a pilgrim says to the traveler at the end of his lecture. "I've noticed that most pilgrims, whether on the Camino or on the road of life, always try to keep up with the others.

"At the start of my pilgrimage, I tried to stay with my group, but I found it too exhausting. I was asking too much of my body. I became very tense and ended up having problems with the tendons of my left foot.

"It got to the point where I couldn't walk for two days, and I realized then that I would only reach Santiago de Compostela if I kept to my own rhythm.

"I took longer than the others, and I had to walk many stretches of the path alone, but I managed to complete the journey by respecting my own rhythm. Ever since, I've applied that to everything else I need to do in life."

PAULO COELHO

CROESUS, THE KING of Lydia, was determined to attack the Persians, but nevertheless, he decided to consult the Greek oracle of Delphi first.

"You are destined to destroy a great empire," said the oracle.

Pleased with this verdict, Croesus declared war. After two days of fighting, Lydia was invaded by the Persians, who sacked the capital city and took Croesus himself prisoner. Outraged, Croesus ordered his ambassador in Greece to go back to the oracle and say that they had been deceived.

"No, you were not deceived," replied the oracle. "You did destroy a great empire: Lydia."

The master says:

The language of signs is there for us to see, to teach us the best way to proceed. However, we often try to distort the meaning of those signs, so that they agree with what we want to do anyway.

MAKTUB

Author Felice Leonardo Buscaglia tells the story of the fourth member of the Magi who also saw the star shining over Bethlehem but who always arrived too late at the places where Jesus might be, because he was always having to stop to help the poor, wretched people begging for his help.

After thirty years following Jesus through Egypt, Galilee, and Bethany, the Magus reached Jerusalem. Too late, the child had already grown to be a man and was being crucified on that very day. The Magus had brought some pearls to give to Jesus but had been forced to sell them to help the people he met on his journey. Only one pearl was left, and the Savior was already dead.

"I have failed in my life's mission," thought the Magus.

Then he heard a voice:

PAULO COELHO

"On the contrary, you kept meeting me throughout your life. I was naked and you clothed me. I was hungry and you fed me. I was in prison and you came to me. I was there in all the poor people you met along the way. Thank you so much for so many gifts of love."

MAKTUB

A SCIENCE FICTION story describes a society in which almost everyone is born ready to perform some task, be it as a technician, an engineer, or a mechanic. A few are born with no special skill, and they are sent to an insane asylum, since the insane are incapable of contributing to society.

One of the inmates rebels. The asylum has a library, and he tries to learn everything he can about science and art.

When he thinks he has learned enough, he decides to escape but is captured and taken to a research facility outside the city.

"Welcome," says one of the people working there. "It is precisely those who are obliged to find their own path whom we admire most. From now on, you can do whatever you want to do because it is thanks to people like you that the world can progress."

Before setting off on a long journey, the businessman said good-bye to his wife.

"You've never given me the kind of present I deserve," she said.

"You ungrateful woman, everything I've given you has cost me years of hard work," said the husband. "What more could I give you?"

"Something as beautiful as me."

The wife waited for her present for two whole years, and when her husband did at last return, he said:

"I finally managed to find something as beautiful as you. I wept over your ingratitude, but I was determined to grant your wish. I've been thinking all this time about what I could possibly give you that would be as beautiful as you, and at last I've found it."

And he held out a small mirror.

MAKTUB

THE GERMAN PHILOSOPHER Friedrich Nietzsche once said: "There's no point arguing about everything; making the occasional mistake is part of the human condition."

The master says:

There are people who are obsessed with being right about every tiny thing. We often don't allow ourselves to make mistakes. All we achieve with this attitude is a fear of moving on.

The fear of making mistakes is the door that keeps us imprisoned inside the castle of mediocrity. If we manage to overcome that fear, we will be taking a big step toward our own freedom.

A NOVICE ASKED Abbot Nisteros in the Scetis monastery:

"What should I do in order to please God?"

The abbot responded:

"Abraham welcomed strangers, and God was pleased. Elijah disliked strangers, and God was pleased. David was proud of what he did, and God was pleased. The tax collector in the temple felt ashamed of what he did, and God was pleased. John the Baptist went into the wilderness, and God was pleased. Jonah went to the great city of Nineveh, and God was pleased.

"Ask your soul what it wants to do. When our soul is in agreement with its dreams, that fills God with joy."

A Buddhist master was traveling on foot with his disciples, when he noticed that they were arguing among themselves as to who was best.

"I've been practicing meditation for fifteen years," said one.

"I've been practicing charity since I left my parents' house," said another.

"I have always followed Buddha's teachings," said a third.

At midday, they stopped beneath an apple tree to rest. The branches were laden with fruit and bent toward the ground beneath the weight.

Then the master spoke:

"When a tree is laden with fruit, its branches bend and touch the ground. In the same way, the truly wise man is one who is humble. When a tree bears no fruit, its branches are haughty and arrogant. In the same way, the fool always thinks he's better than his fellow man."

PAULO COELHO

At the Last Supper, Jesus made equally grave accusations of two of his apostles, and both went on to commit the crimes Jesus had foreseen.

Judas Iscariot realized his error and killed himself. Peter realized his error too, after denying three times everything he believed in.

At the decisive moment, though, Peter understood the true meaning of Jesus's message. He asked for forgiveness and, however humbled and humiliated, carried on.

He could have chosen suicide, but instead he spoke to the other apostles and must have said something along the lines of:

"All right, let people speak of my mistake for as long as the human race exists, but allow me to correct that mistake."

Peter understood that Love is forgiveness. Judas did not.

MAKTUB

A FAMOUS WRITER was out walking with a friend when a boy crossed the road, not noticing a truck heading his way at full speed. In a fraction of a second, the writer had leaped into the path of the truck and managed to save the boy. Before anyone could congratulate him on this heroic deed, he slapped the boy's face and said:

"Don't be taken in by appearances, my child. I only saved you so that you wouldn't escape all the problems you'll have as a grown-up."

The master says:

We sometimes feel embarrassed when we do a good deed. Our sense of guilt is always telling us that, when we act generously, we are actually trying to impress other people, to "bribe" God, and so on. We seem to find it hard to accept that human nature is essentially good. We cover up our kind gestures with irony and indifference, as if love were a synonym of weakness.

PAULO COELHO

He looked down at the table, wondering what best symbolized His time on Earth. Before Him were pomegranates from Galilee, spices from the Southern deserts, dried fruit from Syria, dates from Egypt.

He must have reached out His hand to bless one of those things when it suddenly occurred to Him that the message He brought was for all men in all places, and perhaps pomegranates and dates did not exist in every part of the world.

He looked about Him again and had another thought: the miracle of Creation was there in pomegranates, dates, and other fruit with no need for any human intervention.

Then He picked up the bread, broke it, and gave it to his disciples, saying:

MAKTUB

"Take, eat, for this is My body."

Because bread could be found everywhere, and unlike dates and pomegranates and dried fruit from Syria, bread was the best symbol for the path to God. For bread was the fruit of the Earth *and* of human labor.

THE JUGGLER STOPS in the middle of the square, picks up three oranges, and starts throwing them in the air. People gather round, amazed at the skill and elegance of his movements.

"Life is rather like that," someone says to the traveler. "We always have one orange in each hand, and one in the air. And that's the difference. The orange was thrown into the air with great skill and knowledge, but it has its own path to take. Like the juggler, we toss a dream into the world but don't always have any control over it. We must then surrender it to God and ask that, in due course, the dream may follow its path with dignity and fall, fulfilled, into our hands."

MAKTUB

ONE OF THE most powerful exercises for promoting inner growth consists of simply paying attention to the things we do automatically, like breathing, blinking, or noticing the things around us.

When we do this, we allow our brain to work more freely, without our desires intervening. Certain problems that seemed insoluble end up being resolved; certain jobs that seemed impossible are completed effortlessly.

The master says:

When faced with a difficult situation, try this technique. It requires a little bit of discipline, but the results can be surprising.

A MAN IS selling vases at a market. A woman comes over and looks at the things on sale. Some vases are completely plain, while others have been decorated with meticulous care.

She asks the price of the different vases. To her surprise, they all cost the same.

"How can a decorated vase cost the same as a plain one?" she asks. "Why charge the same for a piece of work that took longer to make?"

"I am an artist," says the seller. "I can charge for the vase I made, but not for its beauty. Beauty comes free."

MAKTUB

THE TRAVELER WAS feeling rather lonely as he left church, then a friend came over to him.

"I really need to talk to you," the friend said.

The traveler saw this encounter as a sign and was so excited that he started talking about everything he considered to be important. He spoke about God's blessings, about love; he said that his friend was a sign that his angel was watching over him because only minutes before he had felt alone, but now he had company.

The friend listened to all he had to say in silence, thanked him, then went away.

Instead of joy, the traveler felt more alone than ever. Later, he realized that, in his excitement to have company, he had paid no attention to his friend's need to talk to him.

The traveler stared down at the ground and saw his words scattered over the sidewalk because the Universe had needed something else at that moment.

PAULO COELHO

THREE FAIRIES WERE invited to the christening of a prince. The first one gave him the gift of finding true love. The second gave him money to spend as he wished. The third gave him good looks.

But—as in every fairy story—a wicked witch appeared. Furious because she hadn't been invited, she put this curse on him:

"Since you already have everything, I will give you even more. You will show great talent in everything you do."

The prince grew up handsome, rich, and in love, but he never managed to fulfill his mission on Earth. He was an excellent painter, sculptor, writer, musician, and mathematician, but he never completed anything because he was so easily distracted and always wanting to do something different.

The master says:

All paths lead to the same place, but choose your particular path and follow it to the end; never try to follow every path.

MAKTUB

AN ANONYMOUS TEXT from the eighteenth century tells of a Russian monk who was looking for a spiritual guide.

One day, he was told that in a certain village there lived a hermit who devoted himself day and night to the salvation of his soul. On hearing this, the monk went in search of that holy man.

"I want you to guide me along the paths of the soul," said the monk.

"The soul has its own path, and your angel will guide you," said the hermit. "Pray ceaselessly."

"I don't know how to pray like that. I want you to teach me."

"If you don't know how to pray ceaselessly, then pray to God and ask him to teach you how to pray ceaselessly."

"You're not teaching me anything," said the monk.

"There is nothing to teach, because one cannot teach faith in the way you can basic math. Accept the mystery of faith, and the Universe will reveal itself to you."

PAULO COELHO

THE SPANISH POET Antonio Machado wrote:

Traveler, you make the path
with your footsteps, nothing more;
Traveler, there is no path,
you make the path by walking it,
by walking it you make the path
and when you look back
you will see the path,
a path you will never walk again.
Traveler, there is no path,
Only the wake left by ships in the sea.

MAKTUB

THE MASTER SAYS:

Write. Whether it's a letter or a diary or a few jottings as you talk on the phone, just write.

Writing brings us closer to God and to our fellow humans.

If you want to have a better understanding of your role in the world, write. Try to put your whole soul into writing, even if no one else will ever read it or, worse, even if someone does end up reading something you didn't want them to read. The mere fact of writing helps us to organize our thoughts and to see the world around us more clearly. A piece of paper and a pen can perform miracles—assuage sorrows, make dreams reality, take away and restore lost hopes.

The word is power.

PAULO COELHO

ACCORDING TO THE desert monks, we must leave the angels free to act. This is why they sometimes did absurd things, like talking to flowers or laughing for no reason. The alchemists follow "God's signs," clues that often make no sense at all but always lead somewhere.

The master says:

Don't be afraid of being called crazy. Do something today that goes against all the logic you were taught. Be slightly less sensible than you have been taught to be. That tiny thing, however tiny, might open the doors to a great adventure—human and spiritual.

A MAN IS driving his very flashy Mercedes-Benz when the tire blows. He tries to change it, only to find that he doesn't have a jack.

"Right, I'll go to the first house I find and ask to borrow one," he says, thinking out loud as he sets off in search of help.

"When the person sees my car, he might want to charge me something for the jack," he thinks. "He could charge me ten dollars. Or possibly fifty, because he'll know I really need that jack. He'll try to take advantage of me and possibly charge me a hundred dollars."

And as he walks, the price goes up and up.

When he reaches the house and the owner opens the door, the man shouts:

"You're a thief, you are! A jack isn't that valuable. You can keep it!"

Which of us can say that we have never done the same?

PAULO COELHO

MILTON ERICKSON WAS the creator of a form of therapy that has recently gained millions of followers in the United States. When he was twelve, he fell ill with polio. Ten months after contracting the illness, he heard a doctor telling his parents:

"Your son won't survive the night."

Then Erickson heard his mother crying, and thought: "Who knows? If I do survive the night, she might not suffer so much."

And he decided he would stay awake until dawn the next day.

In the morning, he called out to his mother:

"Hey, I'm still alive!"

Such was his family's joy that, from then on, he decided

always to live another day and thus spare his parents further suffering.

He died in 1980 at the age of seventy-eight, leaving behind a series of important books on our extraordinary capacity to overcome our limitations.

"FATHER," SAID A novice to Abbot Pastor, "my heart is full of love for the world, and my soul is free of all the devil's temptations. What should be my next step?"

The abbot asked the novice to accompany him on a visit to a patient waiting to be given the last rites.

After comforting the family, the abbot noticed a large trunk in one corner of the house.

"What's inside that trunk?" he asked.

"The clothes my uncle never wore," said the dying man's nephew. "He was always waiting for the right moment to wear them, and they ended up rotting away inside."

"Don't forget that trunk," said Abbot Pastor to the novice when they left. "If you have spiritual treasures in your heart, then put them into practice today. Otherwise, they will simply rot."

MAKTUB

THE MYSTICS SAY that when we set off on our spiritual journey, we tend to talk so much to God that we end up not listening to what He has to say to us.

The master says:

Relax a little. It isn't easy; we have a natural tendency to want to be doing the right thing all the time and believe we can only achieve this by constantly working at it.

It's important to try, to fall, to get up and carry on, but we should allow God to help us. When we're working really hard at something, let us remember to look closely at ourselves and allow Him to reveal Himself and guide us.

And now and then, let us allow Him to sit us on His lap.

PAULO COELHO

A YOUNG MAN came to see the abbot at the Scetis monastery, seeking advice on how to follow the spiritual path.

"For a whole year, always give money to anyone who insults you or behaves aggressively toward you," said the abbot.

For twelve months, the young man did just that, and then he went back to the abbot to find out what his next step should be.

"Go into the city and buy me some food," said the abbot.

As soon as the young man left, the abbot disguised himself as a beggar and, taking a shortcut, hurried to the city gate. When the young man approached, the abbot started hurling insults at him.

"Great!" the young man said to the fake beggar. "For a whole year I've had to pay anyone who was aggressive toward me. Now, though, I can be insulted for free, without spending a penny!"

When the abbot heard this, he removed his disguise.

"You are ready to take the next step, because you can laugh at your problems," he said.

PAULO COELHO

THE TRAVELER WAS walking in New York with two friends. Suddenly, in the middle of a perfectly banal conversation, the two friends started arguing and almost came to blows.

Later on, when they had calmed down, they went into a bar. One of them apologized to the other, saying:

"I've noticed how much easier it is to be hurtful to those we're closest to. I would never have gotten so angry if you were a stranger, but precisely because we're friends, and because you understand me better than anyone, that somehow gave me license to be more aggressive. That's human nature for you."

Perhaps it is, but let's resist it.

MAKTUB

THERE ARE MOMENTS when we would really like to help a particular person, but there is nothing we can do. Either circumstances are against us, or the person is somehow closed off to any gesture of solidarity or support.

The master says:

What's left is love. When we can do nothing else, we can at least love without expecting anything in return or expecting the person to change or even to thank us.

If we do this, love's energy begins to transform the Universe around us. When that energy appears, it always manages to work its magic.

ROMANTIC POET John Keats gave us a fine definition of poetry, and we could, if we chose, take it as a definition of life too:

"I think poetry should surprise by a fine excess, and not by singularity; it should strike the reader as a wording of his own highest thoughts, and appear almost a remembrance.

"Its touches of beauty should never be half-way, thereby making the reader breathless, instead of content. The rise, the progress, the setting of Imagery should, like the sun, seem natural to him, shine over him, and set soberly, although in magnificence, leaving him in the luxury of twilight."

MAKTUB

FIFTEEN YEARS AGO, when the traveler was in denial about his faith, he was with his wife and a friend in Rio de Janeiro. They'd had a few drinks, and then they were joined by another old friend with whom they had shared many an adventure in the crazy 1960s and '70s.

"What are you up to now?" asked the traveler.

"I'm a priest," said the friend.

When they left the restaurant, the traveler pointed at a child sleeping on the sidewalk.

"See how much Jesus cares about the world?" he said with heavy irony.

"Of course," said the priest. "He placed that child right there so that you would see him and realize you could actually do something to help."

PAULO COELHO

A GROUP OF Jewish scholars gathered together to try and write the shortest possible world constitution. If, in the time it took for a man to be able to balance on one leg, someone proved capable of summarizing the laws governing human behavior, he would be considered the greatest sage of all time.

"God punishes the lawbreakers," said one.

The others argued that this wasn't a law, more of a threat, and the law was rejected.

At this point, Rabbi Hillel joined them and, standing on one leg, said:

"Do not do unto others what you would hate them to do to you: this is the whole of the Torah; the rest is mere commentary."

And Rabbi Hillel was thereby deemed to be the greatest sage of his day.

MAKTUB

ON SEEING A huge block of stone in the house of his friend, the sculptor Jacob Epstein, playwright George Bernard Shaw asked:

"What are you going to do with that granite?"

"I don't know yet. I'm still making plans."

"You mean you plan your work?" Shaw responded. "Why, I change my mind several times a day!"

"That's all very well with a four-ounce manuscript," replied the sculptor, "but not with a four-ton block."

The master says:

We all know how we can improve our own work. Only someone with an actual task to perform understands its difficulties.

PAULO COELHO

ABBOT JOÃO PEQUENO thought: "I need to be like the angels, who do nothing but contemplate the glory of God." That night, he left the Scetis monastery and went into the desert.

A week later, he returned. The monk at the gate heard him knocking and asked who it was.

"It's Abbot João," said the abbot. "I'm hungry."

"That's impossible," said the monk. "Abbot João is in the desert, being transformed into an angel. He doesn't feel hunger anymore and doesn't need to work to feed himself."

"Forgive my arrogance," said Abbot João. "The angels help us humans. That is their job, and that is why they contemplate the glory of God. I can contemplate His glory too by doing my daily work."

When the monk heard these humble words, he opened the gate to the monastery.

MAKTUB

Of all the powerful weapons of destruction man has invented, the most terrible, and the most cowardly, is the word.

Knives and firearms leave bloodstains. Bombs destroy buildings and streets. Poisons can always be detected.

The master says:

The word can destroy and leave no trace. Children are controlled for years by their parents, men are pitilessly criticized, and women are systematically massacred by their husbands' comments. The faithful are kept at a distance from religion by those who believe they can interpret the voice of God.

Are you yourself using this weapon? Is this weapon being used against you? If so, don't allow either of those things to happen.

PAULO COELHO

KAREN WILLIAMS IS trying to describe a very odd situation:

"Let's imagine that life is perfect. You are living in a perfect world with perfect people, with everything you could possibly want, with everyone doing everything perfectly and at the right time. In this world, you have everything you could wish for, only what you could wish for, just as you dreamed it might be. And you can live for as long as you like.

"Imagine that, after a hundred or two hundred years, you are sitting on an immaculately clean bench, before some magnificent scenery, and you think: 'How boring! Where's the excitement?'

"At this moment, you notice a red button in front of you, on which is written: SURPRISE!

"Having carefully considered just what this word might mean, do you press the button? Of course! Then you enter a dark tunnel and emerge into the world you are living in right now."

MAKTUB

A DESERT LEGEND tells the tale of a man who was in the process of moving from one oasis to another and began loading up his camel. He loaded on the rugs, the kitchen utensils, and the trunks full of clothes, and the camel stood firm. As he was leaving, he remembered a lovely blue feather that his father had once given him.

He decided to go back and added it to the camel's load.

The camel promptly collapsed under the weight and died.

The man must have thought: "The weight of a feather was too much for my camel."

Sometimes we think the same about those close to us, failing to understand that our jokey comment could be the straw that breaks the camel's back.

PAULO COELHO

"SOMETIMES PEOPLE GET so used to what they see in movies that they end up forgetting the real story," someone says to the traveler, while they're gazing out at the port of Miami. "Do you remember *The Ten Commandments*?"

"Of course. At one point, Moses, played by Charlton Heston, raises his staff, the waters divide, and the Hebrew people cross the Red Sea."

"In the Bible, it's different," says the other man. "There it's God who commands Moses: 'Tell the children of Israel to go forward.' And only once they have started moving does Moses raise his staff and divide the Red Sea, because only by having the courage to follow a path will the path reveal itself."

MAKTUB

THESE WORDS WERE written by the cellist Pablo Casals:

"Each day I am reborn. Each day I must begin again. For the past eighty years I have started each day the same way. This is not a mechanical routine but something essential to my daily life. I go to the piano, and I play two preludes and a fugue by Bach. It is a sort of benediction on my house. But it is also a way of re-establishing contact with the mystery of life, with the miracle of being part of the human race. Even though I have been doing this for eighty years, the music I play is never the same; it always teaches me something new, fantastic, un-believable."

THE MASTER SAYS:

On the one hand, we know that it is important to seek out God. On the other hand, life distances us from Him; we feel ignored by Him, or we're too busy with our daily lives. This makes us feel guilty: we think that we're either giving up too much of our life for the sake of God or that we're giving up too much of God for the sake of our life.

This apparent double-think is a fantasy. God is in life, and life is in God. We only have to be aware of this to have a better understanding of our destiny. As long as we can be in touch with the sacred harmony of our daily life, we will always be on the right path and be able to fulfill our task.

MAKTUB

PABLO PICASSO SAID:

"God is an artist. He invented the giraffe, the elephant, and the ant. He was never trying to follow a style; he was simply doing whatever he felt like doing."

The master says:

When we set off along our path, we are filled with fear; we feel we are obliged to do everything perfectly. Since we each have our own unique life, where does that idea of perfection come from? God made the giraffe, the elephant, and the ant, so why follow a particular model?

The model only serves to show how others define their own realities. We often admire those other models, and we often can't avoid making the same mistakes other people make. But as for living, only we can do that.

PAULO COELHO

SEVERAL DEVOUT JEWS were praying in a synagogue when they started to hear a child's voice reciting: "A, B, C, D . . ."

They tried to concentrate on the sacred verses, but the voice kept repeating:

"A, B, C, D . . ."

They eventually stopped praying, and when they looked behind them, they saw a boy still repeating:

"A, B, C, D . . ."

The rabbi went over to him and asked:

"Why are you doing that?"

"Because I don't know the sacred verses," said the boy. "And I was hoping that if I recited the alphabet, God would take the letters and make the right words."

"Thank you for that lesson," said the rabbi. "I only hope that I can give God my days here on Earth in the same way that you give Him the letters of the alphabet."

MAKTUB

THE MASTER SAYS:

The spirit of God that is present in us all could be described as a movie screen. Various situations appear on it, people fall in love, people separate, treasures are uncovered, distant countries heave into view.

It doesn't matter which film is being shown: the screen remains the same. It doesn't matter if tears are shed or blood, because nothing can sully the whiteness of the screen.

God is there, like that movie screen, behind all the agony and ecstasy of life. We will all see Him when the movie ends.

PAULO COELHO

An archer was walking round a Hindu monastery known for the strictness of its teachings, when he saw the monks in the garden, drinking and having fun.

"How very hypocritical," said the archer out loud. "Those seekers after God's path are always saying how important discipline is, and yet in private, they get drunk!"

"If you were to shoot a hundred arrows one after the other, what would happen to your bow?" asked the oldest of the monks.

"My bow would break," said the archer.

"If someone goes beyond his own limits, that will break his will," said the monk. "If you don't find a balance between work and rest, you will lose your enthusiasm and your way."

A KING SENT a messenger to a distant country bearing a peace agreement to be signed. The messenger revealed the reason for his journey to some friends who had important business dealings with that country. They asked the messenger to stay with them for a few days, and because of the peace agreement, they sent out new orders and changed their business strategy.

When the messenger did finally set off, it was already too late for the peace agreement. War had broken out, destroying all the king's plans as well as the plans of those businessmen who had delayed the messenger.

The master says:

We have only one important thing to do in our lives: to live our Personal Legend, the mission that was given to us. However, we always end up getting weighed down by pointless tasks that eventually destroy our dreams.

PAULO COELHO

THE TRAVELER IS in Sydney, gazing out at the bridge that con-
nects the two parts of the city, when an Australian man comes
over and asks him to read an advertisement in the newspaper
for him.

"It's such small print, I can't read it," he says, "and I've left
my glasses at home."

The traveler has also left home without his reading glasses.
He apologizes to the man, who says, after a pause:

"Oh well, best forget about the advert."

Then, wanting to continue the conversation, he says:

"We're not alone, though. God suffers from poor sight
too, not because he's old, but because he chooses to. That way,
whenever someone close to Him does something wrong, He

MAKTUB

finds He suddenly can't quite see and, not wanting to be un-
just, ends up forgiving them."

"What about the good things people do?" asks the traveler.

"God, of course, never leaves his glasses at home," said the
Australian, laughing and walking away.

"Is there anything more important than prayer?" a disciple asked his master.

The master told his disciple to go over to a nearby tree and cut off a branch. The disciple obeyed.

"Is the tree still alive?" asked the master.

"As alive as it was before," said the disciple.

"Go over there again and cut off the roots," said the master.

"If I did that, the tree would die," said the disciple.

"Prayers are the branches of a tree, whose roots are called 'faith,'" said the master. "Faith can exist without prayer, but prayer cannot exist without faith."

MAKTUB

SAINT TERESA OF Ávila wrote:

"Remember, the Lord invites us all; and since He is Truth Itself, we cannot doubt Him. He said: 'Come to me those who are thirsty, and I will give you to drink.' If His invitation were not a general one, He might have said: 'Come, all of you, for after all you will lose nothing by coming; and I will give drink to those whom I think fit for it.' But as He said we were all to come, without making this condition, I feel sure that none will fail to receive this living water unless they cannot keep to the path."

PAULO COELHO

WHEN ZEN MONKS meditate, they sit down in front of a rock: "Now I will wait for this rock to grow a little," they think.

The master says:

Everything around us is constantly changing. Each day, the sun lights up a new world. What we call routine is full of new ideas and opportunities, but we don't notice that each day is different from the previous one.

Today, somewhere, a treasure awaits you. It might be a little smile; it might be a major conquest—it doesn't matter. Life is made up of miracles small and large. Nothing is boring, because everything is constantly changing. There is no tedium in the world, only in the way we look at the world.

As T. S. Eliot wrote: "We shall not cease from exploration, and the end of all our exploring will be to arrive where we started and know the place for the first time."

MAKTUB

ESSENTIAL COMPANIONS

❖◦❖◦❖◦❖◦❖◦❖

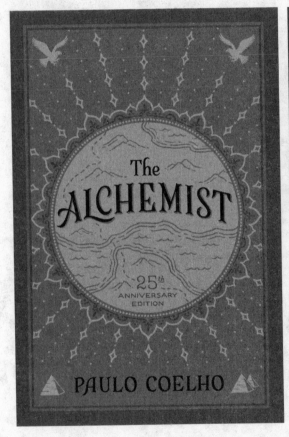

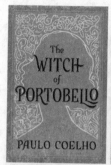

The
WITCH
of
PORTOBELLO

PAULO COELHO

ELEVEN
MINUTES

PAULO COELHO

The
PILGRIMAGE

PAULO COELHO

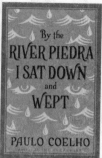

By the
RIVER PIEDRA
I SAT DOWN
and
WEPT

PAULO COELHO

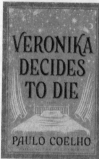

VERONIKA
DECIDES
TO DIE

PAULO COELHO

THE DEVIL
and
MISS PRYM

PAULO COELHO

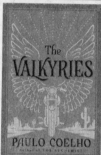

The
VALKYRIES

PAULO COELHO

The
ZAHIR

PAULO COELHO

BRIDA

PAULO COELHO

The
FIFTH
MOUNTAIN

PAULO COELHO

The
WINNER
STANDS
ALONE

PAULO COELHO

THE COLLECTED WORKS OF PAULO COELHO—
FOUND EVERYWHERE BOOKS, AUDIOBOOKS,
AND E-BOOKS ARE SOLD

PROUDLY PUBLISHED BY  HarperOne